D0197364

Encizo saw a flash of steel...

His heart racing, the Cuban's left hand shot out and seized his assailant's wrist. Warrior and enemy struggled fiercely until the Turkish savage rammed a knee into Encizo's groin.

The Cuban gasped as hot agony bolted up from his crotch. The pain whipped along branches of nerves and seemed to claw at his spine. Encizo still held on to the smuggler's wrist to ward off the glinting blade. His other hand raked the Turk's face, desperate fingers seeking an eyeball.

Without warning, a boot tripped Encizo, hurling him to the floor with the smuggler on top of him. The breath was knocked from Encizo's lungs. Lights burst in front of his eyes, and his head seemed to wobble loose from his neck.

He felt his strength slipping, and saw the blade moving slowly closer to his throat.

Mack Bolan's
PHOENIX FORCE

Mack Bolan's
ABLE TEAM

PHOENIX FORCE

Phoenix in Flames

Gar Wilson

A GOLD EAGLE BOOK FROM

WORLDWIDE

TORONTO • NEW YORK • LONDON • PARIS
AMSTERDAM • STOCKHOLM • HAMBURG
ATHENS • MILAN • TOKYO • SYDNEY

First edition November 1984

ISBN 0-373-61314-8

Special thanks and acknowledgment to
William Fieldhouse for his contributions to this work.

Copyright © 1984 by Worldwide Library.
Philippine copyright 1984. Australian copyright 1984.

All rights reserved. Except for use in any review, the
reproduction or utilization of this work in whole or in part
in any form by any electronic, mechanical or other means,
now known or hereafter invented, including xerography,
photocopying and recording, or in any information storage
or retrieval system, is forbidden without the permission
of the publisher, Worldwide Library, 225 Duncan Mill Road,
Don Mills, Ontario, Canada M3B 3K9.

All the characters in this book have no existence outside the
imagination of the author and have no relation whatsoever to
anyone bearing the same name or names. They are not even
distantly inspired by any individual known or unknown to the
author, and all the incidents are pure invention.

The Worldwide Library trademark consisting of the words
GOLD EAGLE is registered in the United States Patent
Office and in the Canada Trade Marks Office. The Gold Eagle
design trademark, the Executioner series design trademark,
the Phoenix Force design trademark, the globe design
trademark, and the Worldwide design trademark consisting
of the word WORLDWIDE in which the letter "O" is
represented by a depiction of a globe, are trademarks
of Worldwide Library.

Printed in Canada

1

Colonel Yakov Katzenelenbogen, the unit commander of Phoenix Force, gazed through the Starlite viewer. He adjusted the light-density level to transform shadows of night into mere dusk. Katz trained the viewer on a small, single-story farmhouse, approximately two hundred yards from his position behind a grassy knoll.

The one-armed Israeli and the other four members of Phoenix Force were ready for battle. They all wore black, night-camouflage uniforms and carried an assortment of firearms and other weapons. Five superbly trained professionals, they comprised the greatest antiterrorist force in the world.

Katzenelenbogen had devoted his life to fighting terrorism. He understood such two-legged jackals as well as any sane man could ever hope to. Katz had been a warrior for more than three decades. It was what he did best.

Katz had fought on many battlefields and had experienced the pain and suffering that war can bring. He lost his right arm in the Six Day War. That same war took the life of his only son. Neither his handicap nor his son's death prevented Katz from continuing down his chosen path. He soon became a full colonel in the Mossad's special antiterrorist section.

Yet Colonel Katzenelenbogen was not to reach the zenith of his career until he was selected to become the team leader of Phoenix Force.

Mack Bolan, better known as The Executioner, had personally chosen Katz and the other men of Phoenix Force. They were the best in the world. A five-man army, Phoenix Force fought the enemies of freedom and civilization wherever the maggots raised their slimy heads to threaten mankind.

Katz continued to gaze through the Starlite. A quiet little farmhouse in southern France seemed an unlikely location for a battle between good and evil. But the men and women at the farm were members of la Brigade rouge. Although smaller and less active than the Italian Red Brigade, the French version of the infamous terrorist organization was equally vicious, ruthless and dangerous.

The terrorists in the farmhouse belonged to a militant Brigade rouge cell led by Jean-Claude Materott. Wanted in four countries for a dozen acts of terrorism, Materott was affiliated with many other organizations in the European terrorist network. His cell had worked with the German Red Army faction, the Italian Red Brigade, Spanish Basque extremists and other fanatic, dangerous groups.

Materott's cell was an international hit team. Their comrades in Germany, Italy and Spain gathered information about certain targets in their own countries, then gave the data to la Brigade rouge. The French terrorists would surreptitiously slip across borders to carry out the hit, then retreat to their home base.

The combined efforts of Interpol and law-enforcement agencies in four nations had been unable to deal with Materott's murderous operation. Recently two U.S. military installations in Europe had been among the sabotage victims of the brigade, and an American diplomat was gunned down by Materott's killers in

Spain. Then the orders came down: the White House had decided it was time to unleash Phoenix Force to deal with the problem.

It had not taken Katz and his team long to locate Materott's base. The Israeli did not think about the events that had led them to the grassy knoll where they would soon launch a midnight raid on la Brigade rouge's headquarters. His mind was concerned only with the task itself.

He observed two men through the Starlite viewer. They carried odd-looking weapons that resembled props from a science-fiction movie—Fusil Automatique MAS rifles, Katz realized.

The French terrorists patrolled the farmhouse. Katz had patiently watched the pair for more than an hour to observe the guard's procedure. The sentries followed a set routine as they walked around the building.

Unprofessional, Katz thought. Proper security required altering guard patrols to avoid patterns that left a site vulnerable to attack. The sentries were poorly supervised and unfamiliar with the basic principles of security.

But Katz did not underestimate his opponents. The men and women in la Brigade rouge were terrorists. Their breed always had to be regarded as highly dangerous.

"Materott managed to steal some fancy hardware for his flunkies," Rafael Encizo whispered as he stared through another Starlite viewer. "But his security isn't very impressive. No electric-eye alarms or mines planted in the area. At least I haven't found any."

The muscular Cuban put down his viewer and broke open a Heckler & Koch 69-A1 grenade launcher to insert a 40mm cartridge into the breech.

Encizo's fighting career began as a resistance warrior

against Communism in Cuba. He later participated in the Bay of Pigs Invasion, where he was captured and imprisoned in Castro's infamous El Príncipe.

Although beaten, tortured and half-starved, Encizo escaped from prison and returned to the United States. He continued to fight for what he believed in—and he believed in Phoenix Force.

The Cuban was ready for combat that night. In addition to the grenade launcher, Encizo carried a 9mm Parabellum Walther MPL submachine gun and a Smith & Wesson Model 59 autoloading pistol in a hip holster. The Cuban had finally accepted the fact that his .380-caliber Walther PPK was not suitable for many combat situations, but he still carried the compact, double-action automatic in a shoulder holster as a backup piece.

"I hope we haven't missed anything," Katz commented.

"Well," David McCarter said, consulting his wristwatch. "I suppose we'll find out in about three more minutes, mate."

The British member of Phoenix Force was eager for combat. A former SAS commando who had seen action in Oman, Vietnam and at the Iranian Embassy in London, McCarter thrived on excitement. If he were ever asked to choose between charging onto the battlefield or going to bed with the most beautiful woman in the world, McCarter would ask the lady to wait until he returned from the fight.

"Manning and James should be in position by now," Katz agreed, glancing at the Rolex attached to the "wrist" of the prosthetic device strapped to the stump of his right arm. "Get ready, David."

"'I was born ready,'" McCarter declared with a wolfish smile.

The Briton was armed with an M-10 Ingram machine pistol and a Browning Hi-Power automatic in a shoulder rig. He kept a .38 Smith & Wesson snubnose in a pancake holster at the small of his back. McCarter's final weapon was perhaps the most unusual—a Barnett Commando crossbow. The Barnett was already cocked, with a bolt ready.

McCarter raised the skeletal metal stock to his shoulder and gazed through the special infrared scope mounted to the frame of the crossbow.

"Do it!" the Israeli told him.

McCarter aimed carefully and triggered the Barnett. The bolt hurled from the crossbow, sliced through the night and found its intended target. The bolt struck one of the sentries in the chest.

The steel tip penetrated flesh and muscle to bury itself in the man's heart. Cyanide oozed from the split fiberglass shaft. The combination of shock and lethal poison killed the sentry before he could utter a sound.

"Merde, alors!" the second guard gasped when he saw his comrade crumple to the ground with the feathered quarrel still jutting from his chest.

Before the man could unsling his weapon or even call out to warn the Red Brigade goons inside the house, a hypo dart stabbed into the side of his neck. The needle sank deeply into his carotid artery and a deadly dose of curare was pumped into his bloodstream. The second guard collapsed next to his slain companion.

Gary Manning and Calvin James advanced from their position a hundred yards west of the farm. Manning carried an Anschutz .22-caliber air rifle. The husky, poker-faced Canadian was the best rifle marksman in Phoenix Force. Playing pin-the-tail-on-the-sentry with a poison dart had been child's play to Manning.

The only native-born American in Phoenix Force, Calvin James was also the newest addition to the elite fighting unit. A tall, long-limbed black man, James had learned how to fight in the streets of Chicago and later as a Navy SEAL in Vietnam. He had been a maverick cop with a San Francisco SWAT team before Phoenix Force recruited him for the war against international terrorism.

James held an M-16 assault rifle with an M-203 grenade launcher attached to the barrel. He covered Manning as the Canadian jogged toward the house.

When the Canadian reached the house, he ducked low to avoid being spotted from a window as he crept to the front door. Manning removed an object that resembled a pack of cigarettes from his shirt pocket. He placed the packet on the top step by the door and pressed a button to activate its battery-operated detonator.

Manning dashed back to James's position. The black commando had assumed a kneeling stance, his M-16 trained on the house. Manning hit the dirt beside him. The Canadian ripped open a canvas pouch on his left hip and removed an M-17 gas mask.

James triggered the M-203. The launcher recoiled against the frame of the assault rifle, driving the plastic stock into James's thigh. A large projectile sailed to the farmhouse and shattered glass from a window.

"Right through the hoop," James said with a chuckle. "Another point for our team...."

The grenade exploded inside the house. Voices shouted and swore in French as a green cloud filled the building. Then the packet at the front entrance exploded. The blast ripped the door off its hinges and tossed it down the steps.

A short distance away, Katz adjusted the straps of an

M-17, using his fingers and the steel hooks of his prosthesis to secure the mask to his head. McCarter had
already discarded the Barnett crossbow and donned his
M-17. The Briton unslung his Ingram and snapped off
the safety catch.

Encizo aimed the H&K 69-A1 launcher at the house
and fired. Another grenade hurled obediently across the
yard and smashed through a window. It exploded,
spewing more tear gas inside the building.

Gary Manning reached the house first. He had abandoned the air rifle, donned a gas mask and unslung a
Heckler & Koch MP-5 machine pistol before he dashed
back to the enemy's lair. The Canadian moved to the
remnants of the door, weapon held ready.

A figure stumbled across the threshold. Coughing violently, the young man pawed both hands at his tear-
stricken eyes. This saved his life. If the terrorist had been
armed, Manning would have shot him down immediately.

Instead the Canadian jabbed the barrel of his machine pistol into the man's solar plexus. The terrorist
doubled up with a wheezing gasp, and Manning clubbed
him between the shoulder blades with the bottom of his
fist. A bent knee rose swiftly and slammed into the
man's face.

As the jackal fell senseless, Manning moved to the
side of the door and took a concussion grenade from his
belt. He noticed McCarter jogging forward to join in
the raid. Manning nodded at his partner and yanked the
pin from his grenade.

As the Canadian tossed the blaster through the doorway, his arm struck another terrorist who was charging
blindly outside. Manning's hand closed on the barrel of
a Soviet-made AK-47 assault rifle. He pulled hard and
swung the gunman off balance.

The terrorist's fingers slipped from the Kalashnikov as she stumbled down the steps. The "gunman" was a slender young woman with long black hair. She blinked her red-rimmed eyes to clear them and snarled at Manning as she reached for a pistol in the waistband of her jeans.

Then the concussion grenade detonated. The house seemed to tremble from the fierce "flash-bang" effect of the explosion. Terrorists inside the dwelling shrieked in pain, and the young woman gasped and recoiled from the burst of light that appeared in the doorway.

McCarter closed in fast. The female terrorist reached again for her pistol, but the Briton's fist lashed out faster and delivered a solid right cross to the jaw. The woman slumped to the ground, unconscious. McCarter plucked the gun from her waistband and tossed it safely beyond her reach.

"You sure have a way with women," Manning remarked, his voice muffled by the filters of his gas mask.

"If she wanted to be treated like a lady," McCarter replied as he moved beside the Canadian, "she shouldn't have become a terrorist."

The Englishman tilted his head toward the doorway. Manning nodded. McCarter then dove inside.

He hit the floor in a fast shoulder roll, and his hurtling form clipped a terrorist's legs and bowled the Red Brigader over. McCarter scrambled for cover amid an atmosphere of confusion, fear and destruction.

Several terrorists, male and female, were already out of action. However, at least half a dozen had not been rendered unconscious by the concussion grenade or the tear gas. Dazed and half-blind, the Red Brigade goons shuffled through the fog of gas that floated inside the house.

Two of the bastards saw McCarter and swung their weapons in his direction. The Briton's battle-honed reflexes responded instinctively. He aimed the Ingram and sprayed the terrorists with a volley of Parabellum rounds. The Red Brigade flunkies hopped and bounced as bullets sizzled through flesh to shatter bones and puncture vital organs.

Manning entered the farmhouse. He saw McCarter scramble to the cover of a sofa while three terrorists opened fire on the Briton's position. The Canadian demolitions expert quickly trained his MP-5 on the trio.

"Non, camarade!" he shouted as loud as the M-17 filters allowed.

The startled trio turned to see another warrior dressed in black, his face concealed by the demon mask with great bug eyes and a hoglike snout. Manning triggered his H&K machine pistol. Full-auto slugs crashed into the hapless terrorists.

Two Red Brigade trash died instantly as bullets chopped into heart and brain matter. The third terrorist screamed as three 9mm slugs ripped chunks of muscle from his right biceps.

A Czech-made Skorpion machine pistol, a favorite weapon of European terrorists, fell from the wounded man's grasp. Panic-stricken, the Red Brigader responded to the most basic instinct of survival—flight. He leaped to the closest window and recklessly dove through what remained of the glass pane.

The terrorist tumbled outside and hit the ground, rolling awkwardly. Pain shot up his wounded arm. The Brigader grit his teeth and managed to climb to his feet.

"Monsieur?" a voice called softly.

The terrorist turned to see Calvin James at the side of the building. The black man had also donned a gas mask before he approached the house. James pointed his M-16 at the startled Red Brigader.

"Don't worry, fella," he remarked, walking toward the terrorist. "You're going to get a kick out of this."

Without warning, James's right leg suddenly swung into a bullet-fast tae kwon-do stroke. His boot smashed into the side of the terrorist's face. The Frenchman seemed to hop backward. Then he fell to earth, unconscious.

The black warrior hurried back to the broken window. He heard the metallic chatter of several full-auto weapons within the dwelling. James cautiously peered through the shattered pane and saw a male and female crouched behind an overturned table. The pair had managed to wrap cloth around their lower faces to screen their nostrils and mouths from the tear gas. They were firing their machine pistols at McCarter and Manning. The British and Canadian commandos had taken cover and conserved ammunition, waiting for a pause in the enemy fire before retaliating.

James thrust the barrel of his M-16 through the window and aimed carefully. He squeezed the trigger gently. A 3-round burst of 5.56mm slugs blasted into the side of the woman's head. Her skull exploded, splashing blood and brains over the male terrorist's shirt.

The Red Brigade goon cried out in horror and alarm. He whirled, swinging his Skorpion toward the black man. James's M-16 rattled out more high-velocity destruction. Two rounds pierced the terrorist's improvised face mask. Teeth and bones shattered. The impact kicked the guy's head back and exposed his throat to a third bullet. The projectile struck a vertebra and severed the man's spinal cord. The savage toppled across the corpse of his female comrade.

A volley of automatic fire erupted from another room. Bullets snapped into the windowsill, inches from James's face. Splinters struck the lenses of his gas mask, the goggles protecting his eyes from shards that might otherwise have blinded the black commando.

"Shit, man," James rasped as he ducked beneath the window.

The terrorists who had fired at the former SEAL were positioned at the narrow doorway of a compact kitchen. Four Red Brigade killers had retreated to the room when the first tear-gas grenade exploded. They did not try to flee out the rear door, certain the house was surrounded.

The brigaders had torn curtains from the windows and wrapped the cloth around their heads and faces to form a crude version of the Kaffiyeh, the Arab headdress. This was the best protection from the gas they could improvise under the circumstances. Two terrorists remained at the doorway, a third guarded the rear entrance, while the fourth man yanked a throw rug from the floor to expose the lid of a trapdoor.

Without warning, an explosion ripped the back door off its hinges. The terrorist stationed next to it was torn to pieces by the blast. His three comrades fell to the floor. One managed to aim his French MAT submachine gun at the door. He hastily opened fire. Bullets hissed through air and traveled harmlessly into the night.

Glass shattered, and the blunt snout of an Uzi submachine gun poked through a window. A salvo of 9mm Parabellum slugs crashed into two startled terrorists before they could realize where the shots came from. Their bullet-shredded bodies slumped lifeless to the floor.

Full-auto flame erupted from the rear entrance. Four 115-grain projectiles struck the last terrorist in the upper torso. The impact sent the brigader's body tumbling across the floor.

The silence of a cemetery followed.

Rafael Encizo entered the house, smoke curling from the muzzle of his Walther subgun. Colonel Katzenelenbogen followed, his Uzi braced across his prosthetic right arm. The Israeli glanced down at the man Encizo had killed.

"Congratulations, Rafael," he told the Cuban. "You got Materott himself. A lot of people will breathe easier, now that he's dead."

"Including me," Encizo admitted.

"Hold your fire!" Katz shouted to the rest of his men. "It's over!"

Calvin James appeared at the rear door. He slipped the strap of his M-16 onto his shoulder and entered. The black warrior exchanged nods with his partners. "Anybody hurt?" he asked. Among his other talents, Calvin James was the unit medic.

"Lots of Red Brigade morons," Encizo replied with a shrug, "but I think all our guys are okay."

The sharp crack of a pistol shot startled the three commandos. Katz and Encizo turned to face the front room, weapons held ready. James cursed under his breath as he drew a .45-caliber Colt Commander from his shoulder leather.

"Relax, mates," McCarter called out. His voice was distorted by the gas mask. Yet everyone recognized it.

"Everything okay, David?" Katz asked.

"Silly bloke was pretending to be dead," the Briton replied. "Pulled a gun on us. Now he won't have to pretend anymore."

"I'd better give them a hand with the survivors," James remarked, reaching for the medical kit at the small of his back. "Probably need to patch most of them up a little, anyway."

"Make it quick," Katz advised. "We want to get out of here before anyone arrives to investigate tonight's disturbance."

"What if any of those turkeys are critically wounded?" James asked.

"Give them some morphine to kill the pain and sedate them," the Israeli answered. "Do what you can, but do it fast. I'll radio Gigene and advise them to prepare to take on wounded parties when they send the choppers in to mop up."

Katz knew quite a bit about the French antiterrorist squad known as Gigene. Phoenix Force had been in touch with Gigene and the Sûreté—the French version of the Central Intelligence Agency. Katz had worked with the Sûreté in the past, and his contacts in French intelligence had helped Phoenix Force locate the Red Brigade lair.

Neither the Sûreté nor Gigene knew much about Phoenix Force, but they realized the five supercommandos had been sent to deal with Materott's assassination cell. Since the French government was notoriously timid about giving approval for aggressive action against domestic terrorism, the Sûreté was glad to let someone else handle the actual raid on the brigade headquarters.

"We'd better make a quick sweep of this place and try to find anything Materott may have kept that could lead to his connections with other terrorist outfits in Europe," Encizo suggested.

"Let's start right here," Katz said as he knelt by the trapdoor. "Materott seemed eager to get his hands on whatever is hidden here."

The Israeli inserted the hooks of his prosthesis into the ring of the trapdoor. He pulled it open carefully, leery of boobytraps. The door was not wired for nasty surprises. Inside he found a metal container. A grenade with a red band around its base sat beside the case. Katz checked again for trip wires before he carefully removed the grenade.

"Thermite," the Israeli said, handing it to Encizo.

"Materott must have put it in there in case he needed to destroy the contents of that container in a hurry," the Cuban mused.

Still careful of traps, Katz pried open the lid of the case. Finding no evidence of trip wires or contraptions, he opened the container and examined the cache with surprise.

The chest was full of small plastic packets of white powder. Katz plucked one of the tiny bags from the pile and turned to Encizo.

"Didn't you work with the U.S. narcotics people a few years ago?" he inquired.

"I helped them bust a smuggling operation in Texas," the Cuban confirmed. "The Mexican Mafia was trying to export heroin to the United States."

"Then you know what heroin tastes like?" the Israeli asked, tossing the packet to Encizo.

The Cuban drew his Gerber Mark I fighting dagger from its belt sheath and slit the plastic bag. He dabbed a finger in the powder and placed it on the tip of his tongue. Encizo spat it out.

"It ain't baking soda," he announced. "I figure that case has about eight kilos of uncut heroin."

"I wonder what Materott intended to do with it," Katz commented.

"Hell, Yakov," Encizo replied. "This stuff is worth

several million dollars to anyone unprincipled enough to sell it.''

"Nobody is going to get a chance to make a penny on it now," the Israeli declared. "When we get ready to leave, we'll destroy this shit ourselves."

"That'll be a pleasure." The Cuban smiled. "That's what I like about Phoenix Force. The work is so satisfying."

"Yeah," Katz agreed simply. "And so necessary."

2

The muezzin called from the minaret of the Mosque of Sultan Ahmet. Down at the harbor, Mohammed Emlet faced Mecca and bowed his head. He did not get down on his knees. The plankwalk was wet and grimy, and Emlet was wearing a white linen suit. Surely Allah would understand his plight and accept the compromise.

Emlet did not like the harbor at Florya Sahil Yolu along the coast of the Sea of Marmara. It was too quiet. Born and raised in Ankara, Emlet did not feel comfortable in Istanbul. Yet Wallach had chosen the pier for their meeting and Emlet had accepted these terms.

A captain in the Turkish National Security Service, Emlet was a sincere patriot, dedicated to protecting his country from enemies, both foreign and domestic. This was his great mission in life and the reason he now waited at the harbor for the American.

Wallach, a CIA case officer stationed in Istanbul, had responded to a coded message sent by Emlet earlier that day. Wallach had then contacted him about the time and place for their meeting. A prompt man, Emlet arrived early and waited for the American to join him.

The sun slowly melted into the sea. Emlet glanced at his wristwatch, although he knew it was still early. He patted the 7.65 mm MKE under his jacket. The world was a dangerous place—especially when one was involved in counterespionage in Istanbul.

At last a figure appeared at the opposite end of the plankwalk. Emlet's eyes had adjusted to twilight. The man who approached was a short, round-shouldered individual clad in a short-sleeved shirt and gray slacks. Emlet frowned and unbuttoned his jacket to allow quick access to his MKE pistol.

"Tunaydin, Efendi Emlet," the stranger announced. His Turkish was better than most foreigners, with barely a trace of accent to suggest he was not a native.

"Isminiz nedir?" the Turk demanded.

"You can call me Mr. Jones," the man replied mildly. "Wallach sent me to meet with you."

"I'm afraid you've mistaken me for someone else, Mr. Jones," Emlet told him.

"Don't be paranoid." Jones sighed. "I work for Wallach. He couldn't make it, so he ordered me to come, instead. He told me you're a serious man and this meeting must be important."

"Why isn't Wallach here?"

"He had a heart attack," Jones answered. "You knew he had to take nitro pills, didn't you?"

"I was aware of that," the Turk admitted. "But what proof can you give me that you and Wallach belong to the same company?"

"What do you want?" Jones growled, growing impatient. "I don't carry a goddamn identification card. Look, Emlet. Why don't you get in touch with Colonel Tursu and have him contact O'Malley at the embassy? Relay your message to the Company that way."

"Too many ears will have an opportunity to hear too much that way," Emlet said grimly. "I'll have to trust you, Mr. Jones."

"I'm listening," Jones said, folding his arms on his chest.

"Due to the nature of my work," the Turk began, pacing along the plankwalk as he spoke, "I've been investigating the activities of the Turkish People's Liberation Army."

"I know." Jones nodded. "And the TPLA is one of the worst terrorist outfits in the world. But they still don't deserve much concern from American intelligence."

"Wallach would disagree," Emlet stated, an edge of anger in his voice. "The TPLA is violently anti-American and anti-NATO. Or don't you recall that Mahir Cayan kidnapped three NATO technicians and murdered them in cold blood before the police killed him in a gun battle by the Black Sea?"

"All right," Jones grunted. "The Liberation Army isn't a nice group of people. We can't argue about that. What's this got to do with this meeting, efendi?"

"My reconnaissance of certain TPLA terrorists led me to a man living in the Haskoy district. He calls himself Viktor Kriviti. He's supposed to be a Yugoslavian refugee who now runs a small watch-repair shop. Actually, Kriviti is a Soviet agent."

"Well," and Jones shrugged, "we all know the KGB has agents in Istanbul and the Russians manipulate some of the terrorist outfits here in Turkey, just as they do in other parts of the world. Naturally the Company is always glad to get information on a *suspected* Soviet agent. I'll advise my superiors to keep tabs on this Kriviti character."

"I haven't finished, Mr. Jones," Emlet told him. "I was a police officer in Ankara before I joined the security service. I contacted some of my informers who have connections with the Istanbul underworld. It seems this Kriviti is involved in the heroin trade. Not opium, mind you, or even hashish. Heroin."

"Drugs?" Jones said with a frown. "Narcotics doesn't sound like the KGB to me."

"You don't understand," Emlet insisted. "The heroin is being shipped out of Turkey to Western Europe and Japan. Perhaps to the United States, as well."

"I don't know much about narcotics," Jones confessed. "But the drug traffic isn't a concern for the CIA."

"But the KGB is involved in shipping heroin to our allies," the Turk stated. "Don't you think that makes it our problem?"

"What proof do you have?" Jones asked. "These informers of yours are criminals themselves, correct? You paid them for information, right? So it's natural for them to tell you exactly what they thought you'd want to hear."

"They don't know I'm with the security service now," Emlet said. "Let's not argue about my sources. Are you going to tell your superiors about this, or not, Mr. Jones?"

"Of course, I'll tell them," Jones assured him, taking a pack of cigarettes from his pocket. "But the Company isn't going to get excited about your theory based on what you've told me tonight."

"Then I'll have to discuss this matter with Colonel Tursu in the morning," the Turk replied. "Sorry to waste your time, Mr. Jones."

"Wait a minute," Jones began as he put a cigarette between his lips. "Have your informers talked to the police?"

"As you pointed out," Emlet said, "they are not the sort of people who like associating with the law. They know me, but I doubt that they'd trust anyone else."

"And you did not ask them about the TPLA or this KGB business?" Jones inquired, fishing a cigarette lighter from a trouser pocket.

"Not directly . . ." Emlet replied.

Jones raised the lighter to the Turk's face and thumbed the wheel. An orange mist sprayed Emlet's nose and mouth. Jones exhaled through the hollow plastic "cigarette" in his mouth to blow the mist directly into the Turk's nostrils.

Emlet smelled almonds. Cyanide gas, he realized. The Turk intel agent reached inside his jacket for the MKE pistol. Jones seized Emlet's arm to prevent him from drawing the gun. Emlet tried to struggle, but his strength faded fast.

Although dizzy and already unable to breathe, Emlet tried to slash a left-hand karate chop at his assailant. Jones shoved the Turk and kicked a foot from the plankwalk to throw Emlet off balance. The Turk fell on his back, but he did not feel the impact of the wooden surface of the pier. The terrible pain in his chest was too great to allow any other sensation.

"Relax," Jones urged almost tenderly. "Your death will be quick. The pain won't last long. There's nothing you can do now except try to die with grace."

Emlet felt the life drain from his body. He was unable to prevent Jones from taking the MKE from his shoulder holster. The assassin calmly tossed the pistol into the sea.

"You're having a fatal heart attack," Jones informed him. "Just like Mr. Wallach had earlier today."

Emlet could not reply. The constriction in his chest seemed to crush his insides. Consciousness threatened to vanish. The Turk resisted the urge to surrender to the peace of death. He prayed that Allah would accept his soul in Paradise.

"I'm sorry." The assassin sighed. "This business can be unpleasant at times."

He watched Emlet tremble with a final muscle spasm. Then the Turk's body finally relaxed. Jones checked for a pulse to be certain his victim was dead.

"Du zvidaniyah," he whispered softly.

3

Hal Brognola struck a wooden match and held the flame to the tip of his cigar. He puffed it gently as he sat at the conference table of the Stony Man war room and gazed at the faces of the five men of Phoenix Force.

Brognola was the man in the middle. He acted as the main link between the White House and all Stony Man operations, which included missions for the elite commando units of Phoenix Force and Able Team.

The fed was also the head honcho of Stony Man. The supersecret organization had originally been conceived as a base of operations for the Executioner's new war against international terrorism. Mack Bolan had formerly fought a successful one-man war against organized crime. Incredibly he had defied the odds and not only survived, but actually triumphed. The Executioner had chopped off the tentacles of the Mafia octopus and hammered its head into the ground.

The Executioner, acting virtually alone, had defeated the mob and left it severely crippled. So who would be a better choice to take on the twentieth-century barbarians of international terrorism than Mack Bolan?

Officially dead, Bolan had received a new identity as Colonel John Phoenix. Stony Man headquarters was the base of operations for Phoenix and his allies. Able Team was created, consisting of three combat specialists who had proven their ability in previous campaigns with Bolan against the Mafia.

The selection of Phoenix Force had been more complicated. Five very special men were chosen from five different countries. They were the new Foreign Legion. Five men who fought like five hundred. They accomplished what armies and governments could not.

Stony Man and Phoenix Force proved to be incredibly successful against terrorism throughout the world. However, the price for success was high.

April Rose, Mack Bolan's woman, and Andrzej Konzaki, the Stony Man weapons expert, were killed in a raid on the headquarters. This was the preamble of a series of events that forced the Executioner to sever his connections with Stony Man and the U.S. government. "Colonel Phoenix" was labeled a renegade. Every major law-enforcement and intelligence network, both East and West, now hunted the Executioner.

The fate of Stony Man was uncertain after Bolan's abrupt departure from the organization. But Hal Brognola still believed in Stony Man. He put his faith in the fighting men of Phoenix Force and Able Team to prove they were still a reliable weapon against the modern-day vandals of destruction.

The warriors did not disappoint their commander. Stony Man was still in business, and the never-ending war against organized evil continued.

"I'm sorry to hit you guys with another mission already," Brognola told the members of Phoenix Force. "I know you could use a little R&R after that assignment in France."

"Who needs to rest after a simple little raid on a bloody farmhouse?" McCarter, the war lover, replied as he lit a Player's cigarette.

"David was just getting warmed up," Gary Manning remarked with a grin.

"It was a pretty easy job compared to the sort of thing we're used to handling," Encizo added. "One little hit and it was over."

"It seems that 'one little hit' was just the beginning of your next job," Brognola stated. "That Red Brigade business was just the tip of the iceberg."

"I was afraid you'd say something like that," Calvin James muttered.

The fed puffed his cigar as he handed a folder to Colonel Katzenelenbogen. The Israeli opened it and glanced over the first sheet.

"This involves that heroin cache we found at the farm," Katz said. "I thought there was something odd about that. Materott seemed more concerned about the heroin than he was about the lives of his comrades."

"French intelligence interrogated the terrorists who survived the raid," Brognola commented. "They didn't have much to say about the drugs. Materott only told them it was part of a scheme against the capitalist bad guys."

"The Corsican syndicate handles most of the narcotics traffic in France," Manning remarked, pouring himself a cup of black coffee. "Maybe Materott had a deal with them."

"The French authorities don't think so," Brognola replied. "And neither does the President of the United States."

"The President?" Encizo raised his bushy eyebrows. "Why is he interested in a cache of heroin in France?"

"Because all evidence suggests the drugs were shipped in directly from Turkey," the fed explained. "According to the survivors of Materott's group, the Red

Brigade got the heroin from a connection with a Turkish terrorist outfit. Probably the TPLA.''

"You mean the Turks sent the raw stuff," Manning began, "but the heroin itself was refined in France."

"That's how the drug business usually operates," Brognola answered. "But somebody's decided to break that tradition."

"Is this a theory based entirely on what some terrorist punks told their captors?" Encizo asked with a frown.

"No," the fed said. "Most of it is based on recent intelligence from Turkey. A National Security agent named Emlet discovered evidence that the Turkish People's Liberation Army has connections with the international narcotics trade. The poppies are grown in Turkey and somebody is processing them into heroin and then shipping it directly to France. We believe they might be sending it to the United States, as well."

"This report says Captain Emlet has disappeared," Katz remarked. "And is probably dead."

"The Turkish authorities haven't found his body," Brognola confirmed. "But they're pretty sure he was killed. Emlet's CIA contact, David Wallach, was found in an alley in Istanbul. At first they thought his death was due to natural causes—Wallach had a history of heart trouble. However, an autopsy discovered traces of cyanide in his lungs."

"Sounds like he was killed by a poison-gas gun," McCarter mused. "Probably disguised as a cigarette lighter or a fountain pen."

"I never heard of terrorists using a contraption like that," Encizo remarked.

"That depends on your idea of what a terrorist is," Katz replied. "But it fits the style of the Morkkrie Dela section of the KGB."

"Huh?" James frowned. "Is that the Soviet assassination group?"

Katz nodded. "Once upon a time it was called SMERSH. Morkkrie Dela sounds less ominous. It means 'wet affairs,' as in 'blood wet.'"

"Or 'get wet,' like we used to say in Nam." The black man shrugged. "Why didn't you just say so in the first place?"

"Christ," Manning muttered. "The KGB has gotten into the dope business."

"Hey," James began, "I've probably seen more pushers and junkies than anybody in this room. After all, I was born and raised in the exotic and colorful environment of a Chicago ghetto and I was a cop for ten years before you guys recruited me for Phoenix Force. Maybe I'm still not familiar with this international-intrigue jazz, but I can tell you dudes this much—the name of the game in narcotics is *money*, man. So why would the KGB get into it? Is the economy so bad in Russia that Moscow has decided to start pushing dope?"

"It's true that most of the narcotics trade is handled by organized crime," Katz explained. "But various governments and clandestine organizations have been involved in it at one time or other. The British were once associated with the opium business in China. This led to the Taiping Rebellion. The British were so eager to control China and the opium trade they actually burned down several imperial palaces in 1860."

"Yeah," Encizo agreed. "And just about everybody has been mixed up with drugs in South and Central America. Both the banana-republic dictatorships and the Communists have peddled dope. Even the CIA got involved with it at one time."

"Okay." James sighed. "That's all depressing as hell, but why would the KGB want to push shit?"

"In the late 1930s," Katz began, "the Japanese managed to covertly control certain tobacco companies in Malaysia and parts of Indo-China. They secretly put opium in many of the cigarettes sold to Asian civilians. Hundreds of unsuspecting people slowly became drug addicts. You can imagine how this could demoralize a society and weaken its ability to defend itself from invading military forces."

"Oh, shit," James gasped. "You think that's what the Russians are up to?"

"You know what the heroin traffic does to people, Cal," Brognola said. "An addict's life revolves around dope. He'll beg, steal or even kill to get another fix. Local police, national law-enforcement agencies and even major intelligence networks are forced to concentrate on stopping the flow of drugs into the country."

"And the more that problem grows, the more everybody has to spend time fighting it." James nodded. "Which preoccupies everybody, so the KGB can do pretty much as it wants. I understand now. Guess that gives me one more reason to hate pushers."

Calvin James's younger sister had died from an overdose of heroin while he was still in Vietnam. The black warrior's mother was also murdered in her apartment—probably killed by heroin junkies. James already had plenty of reason to hate drug dealers.

"How much information did Captain Emlet report to the Turkish authorities before he vanished?" Manning wanted to know.

"Not much," Brognola replied. "Luckily he sent a report to the National Security Council before he arranged a meeting with Wallach. Emlet was a good man. He tried to cover all possibilities."

"In order to learn anything of value we'll have to go to Turkey," Katz stated, lighting a Camel cigarette. "I don't suppose I have to point out the fact that there's a security leak either in the Turkish security service or the CIA operation in Turkey. The KGB has obviously penetrated at least one of their organizations. Perhaps both."

"Yeah," Brognola agreed. "That's why you'll be working with a BND agent named Karl Hahn, who is currently stationed in Istanbul."

The Bundesnachrichtendienst was the federal intelligence service of West Germany, Katz recalled. Phoenix Force had worked with the BND before, when ODESSA Nazis and a splinter group of the Baader-Meinhof gang joined forces to try to seize control of a NATO missile site.

"What is a BND agent doing in Turkey?" Manning asked.

"Well, that's a bit sketchy." Brognola sighed. "A lot of our information abroad is collected on a need-to-know level. The BND doesn't figure we have to know the exact nature of Hahn's mission in Turkey. However, your old friend Colonel Bohler vouches for Hahn."

"Bohler?" Katz raised an eyebrow. "Then Hahn was formerly with the GSG-9 antiterrorist squad?"

"That's right," the fed confirmed. "Hahn has a damn impressive record, too. While he was with the GSG-9 he participated in several missions against the Baader-Meinhof gang, the German Red Army and Turkish terrorists operating in West Berlin. He was transferred to BND because he acquired a habit of hunting down and killing Red Army faction members on his own."

"Sounds a bit unstable to me." Manning frowned.

"He started the vendetta after some members of the Red Army worked over his best friend," Brognola explained. "A fellow GSG-9 agent named Klaus Hausberg. The terrorists tortured the guy, castrated him and gouged out his eyes. Hahn put his pal out of misery by pumping a 9mm through his brain."

"I would have done the same," Katz stated. "Tell me, Hal. Do you know if Hahn just hunted down these terrorists and killed them quickly, or did he torture them first?"

"Hahn referred to it as 'just executions,'" the fed answered. "But he never tortured any of the terrorists."

"Then I'd say he's stable enough," the Israeli announced. "He just likes to do things directly."

"What's wrong with that?" McCarter chuckled.

"Only you would admire somebody with a crazy streak in his nature," Manning muttered.

"Does Hahn speak English?" Encizo wanted to know.

"He was a foreign-exchange student back in the sixties," Brognola answered. "Went to high school in California and studied computer programming at UCLA. Hahn is an electrical wiz and an expert in weapons designs."

"How well does he know Turkey?" Katz asked.

"He's been stationed there for eight years," Brognola replied. "Hahn speaks Turkish fluently. I think he'll be perfect for you guys."

"So long as he agrees to do things our way," Katz commented.

"The guy's sort of a maverick," Brognola said as he smiled. "I don't think you'll have any problem. By the way, according to the rap sheet, Hahn has an uncanny ability to improvise everyday objects to use as weapons in an emergency. He once beat the shit out of a terrorist with a pair of handcuffs. Used them for knuckle dusters. Killed another bastard by cutting his throat with the edge of a broken saucer.''

"Never know when a talent like that might come in handy," Encizo mused. "When do we leave?"

"As soon as you can get ready," the fed answered. "Hahn will be able to supply you with just about anything you'll need, but we've still made arrangements for you to bring whatever weapons and equipment you want to take with you."

"Bloody good," McCarter declared. "I'll pack my Browning, my Ingram and my toothbrush."

"Don't forget the Soviets have already established a damn-good intel network in Turkey," Brognola warned his men. "There's at least one cell of People's Liberation Army terrorists involved, and we can't even guess how many others might be in league with the Russians. The eyes and ears of the KGB will be everywhere. You guys had better be very careful on this assignment, or you'll wind up very dead."

4

The Boeing 747 arrived at the Yesilkoy Airport the following day. Among its passengers were the five men of Phoenix Force. Karl Hahn was waiting for them at the foot of the ramp.

The Phoenix fighters recognized the German agent from a photograph in his BND personnel file. Hahn was a muscular man in his midthirties. He wore a lightweight suit and a cotton shirt open at the throat. A white panama covered most of his dark-brown hair.

"Welcome to Istanbul, gentlemen," Hahn said in greeting, his English bearing only a trace of an accent. "An executive from my firm has spoken quite highly of you. I'm looking forward to our working together."

"Thank you," Katz replied. "I hope our efforts prove most successful."

"A lot of people are counting on that," Hahn said. "Your luggage is being unloaded from the plane. The customs people have agreed to waive inspection of your belongings. Let's get your baggage and discuss business on the way to the safe house."

Hahn escorted the men of Phoenix Force to a Volkswagen minibus. They loaded the luggage into the vehicle and climbed inside. A large, square-shouldered man waited behind the steering wheel. He barely glanced at the newcomers and acknowledged them with a curt nod.

"Don't worry about this vehicle," Hahn assured the

members of Phoenix Force. "We checked for explosives and eavesdropping devices. This wagon is clean."

"What about the driver?" Encizo asked suspiciously.

"Ahmed is an old friend of mine," Hahn replied. "He is very trustworthy."

"He doesn't talk much, does he?" McCarter remarked.

"Ahmed does not talk at all," the German stated. "When Ahmed was five years old his family was slaughtered by Kirmizi Bicak terrorists. They murdered his parents and brothers. Ahmed's sister later died from internal bleeding after being gang raped by the terrorists. The Kirmizi Bicak cut out Ahmed's tongue so he couldn't tell the police what they looked like."

"Jesus," Calvin James rasped. "Were the bastards ever caught?"

"No one ever stood trial for murdering Ahmed's family," the BND agent replied. "But most of the Kirmizi Bicak were killed in battles with the police, the army and rival terrorist outfits."

"Yeah," James commented. "That's one good thing about terrorists... they tend to have a short life span."

"Especially if we have anything to say about it," McCarter added.

The Briton had already worked the combination lock on his aluminum suitcase and now opened the lid. McCarter smiled as he removed the Browning Hi-Power from the case. He examined the pistol carefully to be certain it had not been damaged in transit.

"We haven't exchanged formal introductions yet," Hahn said. "I assume you all know who I am. Of course I recognize Colonel Katz and Gary Manning from Colonel Bohler's descriptions of you, but I'm not sure about the rest of you."

"We're not accustomed to using our real names on a

mission," Katz said. "But I suppose you already know a good deal about us from Bohler."

"I know very little," the German confessed. "Except you five managed to impress Bohler. That isn't easy to do. But I thought one of your teammates was a tall Japanese with an Irish name. Ohara, *ja*?"

Keio Ohara had been one of the original five men of Phoenix Force. He had died bravely in a final battle with the insidious Black Alchemist terrorists.

"Ohara is no longer with us," Katz said grimly.

"I understand," Hahn replied sincerely.

"Hey, David," Encizo said when he saw the Briton slide a 13-round magazine into the butt of his Browning automatic. "I'd like to get my hardware too, amigo."

"Coming up, mate," McCarter replied, handing the Cuban another aluminum case.

"Pass the rest out, David," Katz added.

"You chaps figure I'm the unit batman?" McCarter growled, but he continued to distribute weapon cases to the others.

" 'Batman'?" Calvin James laughed. "Shit. You ain't even Robin, the Boy Wonder, man."

"Do you think it's necessary to get those weapons ready now?" Hahn inquired. "After all, we're still in the airport. We haven't even reached the main terminal at Sishane yet."

"Airports are hardly immune to terrorist attacks," McCarter remarked, loading his M-10 machine pistol. "Remember what happened at Lod Airport about ten years ago? Or the bomb attack at the London airport last year?"

"And we've been attacked in airports before," Manning added as he inspected some detonators for his plastic explosives. "Once in Japan we barely got off the plane before we were surrounded by terrorists."

"That's not going to happen here," Hahn assured him.

"You can't be too careful in this business," Calvin James commented. He unfolded the metal stock to a Smith & Wesson M-76 submachine gun and shoved a 32-round magazine into its well.

"All right," Hahn said with a sigh. "But we've kept your mission top secret. Nobody knows why you're in Turkey...."

Hahn's words were cut short as a wall of fire suddenly exploded in front of the minibus. Projectiles rung sourly against metal, accompanied by the harsh bark of pistol shots. The men of Phoenix Force immediately hit the floor, weapons in their fists.

"Nobody knows about us, huh?" Encizo rasped, working the bolt of his Walther MPL subgun.

"Maybe Ahmed ran a stop sign," McCarter sneered. "Bloody tough traffic cops you've got in this country."

"Work on your joke book later," Katz snapped, chambering a round into the breech of his Uzi. "How solid is this bus, Hahn?"

"Very," the German replied through clenched teeth. He had drawn a Walther P-5 automatic from a shoulder holster. "Armor plated and bullet-resistant glass."

Ahmed stomped on the gas pedal. The Volkswagen bolted forward. Figures dressed in shabby clothing and crude stocking masks leaped out of the path of the charging minibus. They angrily shouted and cursed as they fired handguns at the vehicle.

"I'll cover the back door," Manning volunteered.

"Me, too," Encizo added.

The Canadian and Cuban commandos moved to the rear of the bus. McCarter was already in position by a side door, his Ingram held ready. James stationed himself at another side entrance.

Katz raised his head long enough to glance out the windows. Some flames still danced along the windshield. The enemy had probably hit the VW with a Molotov cocktail. Crude, but deadly.

All the terrorists appeared to be armed only with handguns. Katz did not see any automatic weapons or shotguns in the hands of the aggressors. The terrorists' tactics seemed as unsophisticated as their weaponry. They had simply surrounded the vehicle and attacked, firing their pistols at the minibus.

"Scheisser," Karl Hahn rasped, staring through the windshield.

Ahmed nodded in agreement. A baggage cart with a caterpillar of metal wagons attached blocked the path of the minibus. Apparently the driver of the cart had hastily abandoned it when the shooting began. He had picked a hell of a place to park it.

Ahmed tried to avoid the cart. He turned the wheel hard and swung the VW to the left, but the nose of the bus crashed into one of the wagons. Suitcases, trunks and duffle bags hurled in all directions. The wagon flipped on its side and took others linked to it to the ground. Even the cart tipped over.

The front tires of the bus caught on the rim of a wagon. Ahmed tried to drive over the obstacle, but the VW refused to move. The terrorists cried out in victory as they charged the disabled vehicle.

"That tears it," Gary Manning muttered as he rolled down a window to thrust the barrel of his machine pistol through the gap.

Three terrorists closed in rapidly. Two fired pistols at the bus while their comrade set fire to a rag stuffed in the neck of a bottle. Manning aimed carefully and squeezed the trigger of his H&K blaster.

A trio of 9mm slugs hit the firebug in the chest like a copper-jacketed sledgehammer. The impact slammed him to the ground. He still held the Molotov cocktail in his fist. Flame reached gasoline. The bottle bomb exploded like a grenade.

Fiery liquid instantly splashed over the other two terrorists. The pair shrieked in agony as they tumbled to the ground, their bodies shrouded in flame. Manning terminated their suffering—and their lives—with a volley of 9mm mercy rounds.

The remaining terrorists retreated in horror from the burning corpses of their comrades, but they stubbornly continued the assault on the minibus. They attacked both sides of the vehicle. Spiderweb patterns appeared in the glass panes. The bullet-resistant glass would soon fall apart.

Calvin James had also opened a window wide enough to poke the barrel of his M-76 outside. The 9mm Smith & Wesson chatterbox was a favorite weapon of the SEALS, and James and the M-76 were old combat friends. "Battlefield soul mates," as the black warrior sometimes referred to a weapon he trusted.

James's attention centered on a terrorist armed with an American-made Colt 1911A1 pistol. The Turkish lowlife had converted the pistol to fire full-auto. A 15-round, extended magazine jutted from the butt of the modified handgun.

None of these alterations helped the terrorist one iota. The Colt pistol had not been designed to fire full-auto. The recoil of the .45-caliber weapon was more than the Turk could handle. He fired more rounds into the sky than at the bus.

James watched the Turk's arms rise with the climb of the modified pistol. Then he shot the lunatic. The terrorist suffered cardiac arrest when two Parabellum missiles ripped through his heart.

The black badass immediately trained his M-76 on another aggressor. The terrorist dropped to a kneeling stance and aimed his pistol at the bus. Calvin James triggered his subgun. A column of 9mm bullet holes split the fanatic's face from nose to forehead.

"This is a goddamn turkey shoot," James yelled.

He swung the M-16 toward a third terrorist, who had decided to throw himself to the ground. James nailed the guy with a salvo of bullets that ripped into the Turk's rib cage. The terrorist screamed and tried to roll away from the line of fire. Instead he rolled right into the path of another burst of 9mm death from Encizo's Walther machine gun.

Rafael Encizo had decided to risk opening the rear door after the terrorists retreated from the Molotov cocktail explosion. Manning covered Encizo as the Cuban cautiously ventured outside.

The terrorists at the side of the bus were too concerned about being shot by Calvin James to notice Rafael Encizo. The Cuban suddenly announced his presence by blasting two Turkish fanatics with his submachine gun. Parabellum slugs knifed through one terrorist's backbone and snapped his spinal cord. The other Turk turned sharply, only to catch two bullets in the throat.

Violently choking and spitting blood, the wounded terrorist fell to his knees. Encizo finished him off with another volley. Three stray MPL rounds struck the man who had rolled away from Calvin James's gunfire.

Katz and McCarter were ready for the terrorists who attacked the opposite side of the bus. The Israeli and British commandos trained their weapons on the enemy and opened fire. The 9mm projectiles slashed into three Turkish assassins.

Bullet-torn bodies crumbled to the ground. Two aggressors swung their weapons toward the windows to return fire. However, the rest of the terrorist gang realized they were no match for the warriors within the minibus. They desperately dashed for the shelter of the closest building.

"The *Schweinehunden* are getting away!" Karl Hahn announced as he reached for a door handle with his left hand. His right was still fisted around the grips of his Walther P-5 pistol.

"Wait!" Katz warned. "There are still a couple of them by the bus."

"I'll pin the bastards down," McCarter declared. "You chaps go after the rest of the bastards."

The Briton fired a long burst of full-auto rounds at the two terrorists who elected to continue the assault on the bus. The pair had moved to the overturned luggage cart for cover. The terrorists ducked low as McCarter's Ingram pelted the cart with 9mm slugs.

"Now!" Katz told Hahn.

The German swung open the door and leaped outside. Katz followed, his Uzi braced for combat. Half a dozen terrorists had retreated to the entrance of a gate marked BAGAJA: TASIT GIREMEZ. Katz and Hahn swiftly pursued their quarry.

The two Turkish gunmen hidden behind the cart rose up and aimed their pistols at Katz and Hahn. But before either man could squeeze a trigger, McCarter fired his Ingram. Two Parabellum missiles sliced into the side of an opponent's head. The top of his skull erupted like a baby volcano. Bone chips and slimy brain matter burst from the exit wound above his hairline.

Furious, the surviving terrorist aimed his MKE automatic at McCarter's position. The Briton ducked under the window frame of the side door. Two bullets struck reinforced glass. It cracked and shattered, and pieces of broken glass showered McCarter's arched back and shoulders. A stray 7.65mm slug buried itself in the backrest of a passenger's seat.

"I hope they make you pay for that window, bloke," McCarter growled through clenched teeth.

The terrorist indeed paid . . . with his life. Ahmed, the mute driver, hopped outside while the gunman was busy shooting at McCarter. The big Turkish agent quickly aimed a Government Colt pistol at the terrorist. He squeezed off two shots. Both .45-caliber projectiles smashed into the aggressor's upper torso, and the impact pitched his body five feet. The terrorist hit the pavement in a quivering, dying heap.

"Anybody manage to take any prisoners?" Gary Manning called out to the others.

"Hey, man," Calvin James replied as he loaded a fresh magazine into his M-76. "You gotta be kidding."

5

"Suraya bakin!" an airport employee cried out, pointing at the group of armed invaders who burst into the baggage-reception section.

The survivors of the terrorist hit team had fled into the building. They had no plan of action except simple survival. The unarmed baggage crew shared this concept. They bolted for the nearest exit and prayed the gunmen would not follow them.

Two terrorists, armed with Yugoslavian Model 57 autoloading pistols modified to full-auto and equipped with extended 20-round magazines, stationed themselves at the gate entrance. The other four fanatics darted inside and moved between columns of luggage racks, seeing an escape route.

"Amerikan domuz!" a terrorist sentry snarled when he saw Karl Hahn charge toward the gate.

The German dove to the ground before the two lunatics opened fire with their modified machine pistols. A swarm of 7.65mm bullets sizzled through the air above Hahn's prone figure.

More full-auto fire erupted as Yakov Katzenelenbogen triggered his Uzi submachine gun. One terrorist received a lethal dose of 9mm lead poisoning that snuffed out his life like the flame of a candle. The other sentry cried out as two Parabellums punched through his left biceps and shattered the elbow joint.

The terrorist staggered but did not fall. Although his broken arm hung uselessly at his side, the maniac still held the converted M-57 pistol in his right fist. He tried to aim it at the Israeli war-horse.

Karl Hahn ruined the terrorist's plan. He adopted a prone pistol stance, aimed the Walther in a two-hand Weaver's grip and opened fire. The double-action pistol barked three rounds, and the terrorist collapsed as a trio of bullets drilled through his chest. The modified M-57 slipped from his lifeless fingers.

Katz and Hahn reached the gate. The Israeli pressed himself against the door frame. He glanced at Hahn. The German jerked his head toward the entrance and tapped himself on the chest. Katz nodded.

Hahn ducked low and lunged across the threshold. He hit the floor in a fast shoulder roll while Katz swung the Uzi around the corner. No terrorists were waiting to ambush them.

The German scrambled to the cover of a pillar. He held the Walther pistol ready to defend Katz as the Israeli jogged to a forklift for shelter. Both men waited, listening and watching for any sign of the remaining terrorists.

"Dur! Polis!" a voice shouted from the opposite end of the room.

A young man dressed in a blue uniform and cap had entered the baggage area via another door. The Turkish policeman had managed to get the drop on two terrorists. He aimed an MKE pistol at the pair and ordered them to throw down their weapons. The terrorists obeyed.

Pistols cracked. The policeman's body jerked violently as bullets crashed into his chest. The two missing terrorists appeared from their hiding place behind a column of luggage racks. One of the brutes laughed as he stepped closer and aimed a Makarov pistol at the wounded cop.

The young officer was tough, and he still had his gun in his hand. The MKE autoloader barked twice. The sadistic gunman's head recoiled when two 7.65mm slugs slammed into his face. But the other terrorist pumped two more rounds into the policeman, and the cop's body slumped limply to the floor.

Katz and Hahn closed in fast. The Israeli fired his Uzi as he ran. The terrorist who had killed the cop screamed and dropped his pistol. His right arm had been pulverized by three Parabellums. A fourth slug shattered his collarbone.

The wounded terrorist fell backward into his two unarmed comrades. One Turkish barbarian caught his injured friend while the other goon tried to retrieve his fallen weapon.

"Yok!" Hahn shouted, pointing his Walther at the trio. *"Anladiniz mi?"*

The two uninjured terrorists raised their hands in surrender. Their wounded partner stood unsteadily between them, his face contorted by pain. Katz and Hahn approached cautiously, weapons held ready.

"Hareket etmek degil!" Hahn snapped, warning the terrorists not to move.

"Peki," one of the Turks agreed with a nod.

"Affedersiniz," another terrorist began in an apologetic tone. *"Lutfen daha yavas konusur...."*

The Turk did not complete his request. Instead he shoved his wounded comrade, sending the bloodied, helpless figure hurtling toward Katz and Hahn. The man collided with the German agent, striking the Walther from Hahn's grasp.

Katz was not taken off guard by the terrorist's tactic. Although his knowledge of Turkish was limited, the Phoenix Force commander recognized the word *lutfen* —"please." He knew terrorists well enough to be suspicious of one who seemed too polite.

One of the goons lunged forward and lashed out a foot, trying to kick the Uzi from Katz's hand. The Israeli easily avoided the terrorist's kick. His prosthetic arm shot out, and steel hooks snapped shut around the Turk's ankle.

Katz quickly launched his own kick. The steel toe of his shoe crashed into the terrorist's genitals. A high-pitched whine escaped from the Turk's throat. Katz twisted the guy's ankle hard. The steel hooks pulled away muscle and snapped bone. The Phoenix Force veteran released his opponent and let the man drop senseless to the floor.

The third terrorist pulled a switchblade knife. A 6-inch blade snapped open as he attacked Karl Hahn. The German dodged the first knife thrust. The Turk quickly slashed his blade at Hahn. Again the BND man leaped out of range.

Hahn plunged both hands into his jacket pockets as the Turk closed in for the kill. The German's right hand flashed and hurled a small metal object that hit the terrorist in the face. The man grunted, more startled than hurt by the tactic.

However, the Turk was distracted long enough for Hahn to strike out with the plastic object in his left fist. He raked it across the back of the terrorist's hand. Blood oozed from a shallow cut. The switchblade fell from numb fingers.

Hahn rammed his right fist under the guy's rib cage and drove the end of his little plastic weapon into the

facial nerve under his jawbone. The dazed terrorist staggered backward. Hahn delivered a fast, short karate
punch to the point of his opponent's chin. The Turk's
eyes rolled upward and he fell unconscious at Hahn's
feet.

Katz picked up the object Hahn had thrown in his adversary's face. It was a cigarette lighter. He handed it to
the German.

"You dropped this," Katz told him.

"Danke," Hahn replied as he knelt beside the senseless terrorist. He used the man's shirt to wipe blood
from the plastic teeth of his comb.

"Your file was correct," the Israeli remarked. "You
do have a talent for improvised weapons."

"I just don't like breaking my knuckles," the German said with a grin. "Well, we have a couple of live
prisoners, Colonel."

"Yes," and Katz nodded. "I just hope we can get
some answers out of them."

THE ISTANBUL POLICE soon arrived at the airport in full
force and armed to the teeth. Fortunately Hahn's position with the West German embassy granted him diplomatic immunity. He also had a number of connections
in high places, both in Istanbul and in the capital city of
Ankara.

After several phone calls and a conversation with the
Istanbul police commissioner, Hahn persuaded the
authorities that he and his five mysterious companions
had acted in self-defense. He also convinced them to re-
lease a slightly altered version of the incident to the
press.

Most of the members of the terrorist hit team at the
airport were easily identified as political extremists who

had already been under surveillance by various Turkish law-enforcement and national-security organizations. This fact reinforced Hahn's claims that the formidable strangers were on a top-secret mission that was in the best interests of the free world in general and Turkey in particular.

The authorities agreed to cooperate. Turkey had had more than its share of civil unrest and terrorist activity. Since World War Two, Turkey had been on the brink of anarchy and civil war on three occasions.

Conflicts between the democratic party, the agas and various would-be revolutionary groups triggered a bloodless military coup d'etat in 1960. The Turkish army declared martial law until the country was stable enough for elections. Then the military stepped down.

Turkey was ruled by a civilian government for a decade before violence and terrorism forced the army to again seize control of the nation. Once again the military restored order, arranged for elections and relinquished command to the new government.

However, the worst period of domestic violence was yet to come. Terrorism reached a horrifying peak. Sabotage, bombings and murder became everyday activities. Often it was difficult to determine whether a left-wing or right-wing group was responsible for a particular terrorist act. Many extremists were such total fanatics they would kill individuals of similar political beliefs simply because he or she failed to live up to their notions of "dedication to the cause." Some terrorists were less than fifteen years old. They committed acts of incredible violence for reasons they could neither explain nor begin to understand. Anarchy, if not total madness, seemed destined to triumph in Turkey.

Then, in 1980, the military stepped in for the third

time. The government and the economy gradually stabilized. Turkey made a remarkable recovery. General Evren, formerly the Chief of Staff at the National Security Council, was elected president by a landslide by ninety percent of the voters. Evren knew Turkey and he understood his nation's problems.

Terrorism remains one of Turkey's major concerns. Some critics have unfairly blamed this domestic violence on the "violent nature" of Turks themselves. This theory is based on ethnic prejudice more than fact. Many of Turkey's internal troubles actually stem from external sources.

Turkey is surrounded by Greece, Bulgaria, Syria, Iraq, Iran and the Soviet Union. Greece and Turkey are not on friendly terms due to the long and bitter dispute concerning the island of Cyprus. The other five neighboring countries have all been involved in the vicious business of exporting international terrorism, especially the puppet masters in the Kremlin and the KGB.

The infamous George Habbash and Wadi Haddad, the leaders of the most militant Palestinian terrorist groups, recruited hundreds of young Turks. They were trained in the arts of destruction in Iraq and shuffled back into Turkey via Diyabakir.

When Viktor Sakharov defected in 1971, the reason for this covert recruiting by Habbash and Haddad became clear. Terrorism in Turkey did not help any Palestinian cause, but it served the interests of the KGB by causing unrest within a non-Communist nation at the very borders of the Soviet Union.

The KGB's Department "A," sometimes called the Department of Disinformation, had also been busy circulating forged documents that accused America of conspiring with Greece to seize control of Cyprus. This "black propaganda" campaign was very successful. Hostility against the United States increased in Turkey. So did the incidents of terrorism.

After decades of political violence and unrest, Turkey had finally achieved some measure of law and order. The government did not want another outbreak of wide-spread terrorism. If the five mystery men with Karl Hahn could help prevent this from happening, then they were more than welcome in Turkey.

HAHN LED PHOENIX FORCE to a radio shop located on Milet Caddesi near the Column of Arcadius. A sign on the door claimed the place was closed for renovation. In reality, the shop was Hahn's safe house. The back room housed a miniature communications center complete with a sophisticated computer system. The basement had been converted into a small billet with bunk beds, kitchen and a well-stocked food supply.

"You wanted some answers, Colonel," Hahn told Katzenelenbogen after scanning the viewscreen of his computer. "I've got some for you, but I don't think it will help us."

"Let's hear them, anyway," the Israeli replied.

"This computer is linked with terminals at the Istanbul Police Department and the National Security Service in Ankara, which is also the Turkish branch of Interpol," Hahn explained. "Both sources have transmitted information about the terrorists who attacked us at the airport. They were all members of SAWI—Students Against Western Imperialism."

"Are they connected with the Turkish People's Liberation Army?" Gary Manning inquired.

"No," Hahn answered, shaking his head. "SAWI is a small, very militant outfit that is violently anti-

American. Apparently they attacked us simply because you five arrived in a plane from the United States.''

"Just a coincidence?" Rafael Encizo frowned. "Maybe SAWI isn't connected with the TPLA, but the Russians are probably pulling a few strings with those junior terrorists, too."

"They probably are," the German agreed. "But I'm certain the KGB would not have sent such poorly trained and poorly armed young zealots to dispatch someone they considered a serious threat to a major clandestine operation."

"I agree, Karl," Katz stated. "If the KGB suspected why we're in Turkey they would have sent professionals. One man with a rocket launcher could have blown that bus to pieces—and us with it."

"Okay," Calvin James remarked, slipping into his Jackass leather rig housing the Colt Commander. "So our cover is still solid. That's nice. Now what do we do?"

"We get on with our mission," Katz replied. "Captain Emlet mentioned a Yugoslavian watch-repair shop owner in his last report. He thought this man was connected with the heroin operation. Did the Turkish security service look into this?"

"Viktor Kriviti, or whatever his real name is," Hahn began, "disappeared about the same time Emlet vanished. No one was too surprised. The KGB must have guessed Kriviti's cover was burned. Turkish intelligence took the watch shop apart, looking for evidence that might help in this case. They didn't find a thing. Kriviti was a careful man."

"The KGB are professionals," Katz remarked. "We can't count on them making very many mistakes."

"But terrorists usually aren't that careful," Manning

added. "Emlet was following a TPLA fanatic named Kerim Balkon, right? Maybe he's the key."

"The NSS already thought of that." Hahn sighed. "Balkon has also disappeared."

"Seems to be a lot of that going around these days," McCarter muttered sourly.

"This is Istanbul, my friend," the German said with a shrug. "Intrigue and espionage have been a tradition in this city for centuries. People vanish all the time here."

"I'm still learning this cloak-and-dagger stuff," James admitted. "But I know something about police procedures. If you can't find one lead, you look for another. And another and another. Emlet kept tabs on Balkon for a long time. The son of a bitch must have associated with other low life besides the Yugoslavian."

"Good point," Hahn agreed. "I'll see what the computer tap has on Emlet's previous reports about Balkon's activities."

The German fed questions into the computer. The machine responded rapidly. The screen was suddenly covered with columns of numbers and key letters. Hahn activated a deciphering device to translate the coded message.

"We have a list of Balkon's associates according to Emlet," Hahn declared. "Kriviti's name appears frequently, but so do a number of others. Especially Hussein Ali Yazod."

"Who's he?" Encizo inquired.

"I'll know in a minute," Hahn replied, his fingers dancing across the keyboard of the computer console.

In a moment Encizo had his answer. Hussein Ali Yazod was an Iranian who fled to Turkey in 1971 to escape SAVAK, the Shah's secret police. He was employed on the assembly line of a furniture factory owned by Dimitri Sandalye, who was known to be an outspoken critic of the current Turkish government and a supporter of something called "modified Marxism."

Turkish security and the Istanbul police suspected Sandalye might be involved with certain political extremists, but they found nothing to support this belief. The authorities also suspected Yazod of participating in a number of crimes, including the murder of an Istanbul police officer. The cops hauled in Yazod more than once, but they could never prove he was guilty of anything more serious than bad manners.

"Yazod sounds like a promising lead to me," James said. "Where can we find this Iranian *pissant?*"

"At the Sandalye factory," Hahn replied. "Yazod and several other employees actually live there."

"We may have found a bloody nest of terrorists already," and McCarter smiled, delighted by the possibility.

"Donnerwetter," Hahn groaned. "You can't just launch a raid on that factory without any grounds for—"

"The proof is probably waiting for us there," Katz said simply. "We'll see what we can find tonight."

" 'Tonight'?" Hahn rolled his eyes toward the ceiling. "You don't believe in wasting time."

"We'd rather waste terrorists," James replied with a smile.

6

Major Mikhail Vissarionovich Borgneff gazed out the window at the mountain peaks beyond. The Union of Soviet Socialist Republics lay at the opposite side of those mountains. Borgneff longed to return to his homeland.

Yet unlike most Russians Borgneff did not feel a great emotional attachment for his country. He did not love Russia or care much about her people. Borgneff was not truly dedicated to the glorious cause of the Communist Party, either. Of course, he gave lip service to the cause and he never openly questioned orders.

Borgneff's reason for missing the Soviet Union was simply because he preferred to operate within his own country. His reasoning was simple: it is easier and safer to conduct covert missions on your own turf than that of foreign lands.

The Komitet Gosudarstvennoi Bezopasnosti roughly translated meant the Committee for State Security. The KGB was the largest intelligence network in the world. Yet only ten percent of all KGB activity was conducted outside the Soviet Union.

The majority of KGB operations were carried out within the U.S.S.R. Soviet spies spy on Soviet citizens. The Kremlin was fearful of anything it could not control, so it did its best to control the actions of the Russian people. Nothing worried Moscow more than free thought among its own subjects. Thus the KGB watched, harassed and intimidated the Soviet people.

Borgneff did not question this practice. He did not worry about the morality of Siberian labor camps or recruiting children to inform on their own families. It did not disturb him that Moscow twisted the truth and printed lies in *Pravda*, or that the KGB practiced subversion, sabotage and murder in foreign lands. After all, this was done within the Soviet Union, as well.

Borgneff was not concerned with morality because he actually liked his work. He enjoyed the privileges and power that belonging to the KGB bestowed. Borgneff saw nothing wrong in this. He had been recruited into the KGB when Nikita Khrushchev was premier, and he had become quite comfortable with his work.

However, at the age of forty-five, Borgneff did not like taking risks anymore. Operations within the U.S.S.R. were relatively simple and safe. Missions beyond the Iron Curtain were another matter entirely.

Borgneff was particularly unhappy about his current mission in Turkey. He cursed himself for having learned to speak and write Turkish fluently. Why had he not mastered French or German, instead? Borgneff did not like Turks, whom he considered totally uncivilized. He especially disliked Turkish terrorists. Yet his assignment forced him to deal with them.

The KGB officer sighed as he stared at the mountain known as Buyuk Agri Dagi. If the mission went well, he would return to the Soviet Union. Borgneff had been promised a promotion to second in command of the Internal Investigations Department in Kiev. He would never be forced to leave Mother Russia again. For Borgneff, this was all the motivation he needed.

"You seem deep in thought, Major," Mustafa Kaplan commented as he approached Borgneff. "I hope nothing troubles you."

"Not at all," the Russian assured him. "Everything is proceeding as planned."

"Until recently," Kaplan said grimly.

The Turk's reptilian eyes stared down at Borgneff. Kaplan was almost seven feet tall, but his towering frame was painfully thin. Sunken cheeks, bloodless lips and deep-set, dark eyes created a corpselike face. Borgneff wondered how a man so full of death could have four healthy sons.

"Are you still worried about those two agents I killed?" Borgneff inquired. "Any problem they may have presented died with them."

"I do not share your confidence, Major," Kaplan confessed. "Agent Emlet had been studying the movements of the People's Liberation Army for months. He must have reported information about more than the location of the watch-repair shop."

"We've got people planted inside the National Security Service and the American CIA," the KGB man said with a shrug. "They've already examined Emlet's reports. I assure you, there is nothing to worry about."

"That is not good enough, Major," Kaplan insisted. "These terrorist trash have connections throughout Istanbul. There are too many of them for you to hide them all from the eyes of the authorities. I never approved of using such people. They are fanatics. Emotional fools who tend to become careless."

"But they are blindly dedicated to the cause of international revolution," Borgneff said. "And the TPLA are better trained than those common thugs on your payroll."

"Those thugs are familiar with the narcotics underworld," the Turk declared. "They might not be trained in blowing up school buses or shooting police officers in the back, but they are far more professional than any of your terrorist puppets.''

"We should not argue about this matter," the Russian said. "We need both your syndicate sources and the terrorists, if this mission is to succeed.''

"So you have said before," Kaplan replied as he strode across the library to his desk.

Bookcases filled with leather-bound volumes surrounded the two men. Borgneff had noticed titles written in seven languages, including Russian and English. The subjects covered by Kaplan's books ranged from religion and international politics to poetry and Ottoman art. Yet history seemed to be the Turk's primary interest.

One cabinet was filled with biographies of men Kaplan admired. Alexander the Great, Julius Caesar, Napoleon, Emperor Constantine and Adolf Hitler were all among his heroes. Yet other names appeared. Rothschild, Rockefeller, Hughes, Onassis and others associated with wealth and power.

Kaplan sank into a leather armchair behind his hand-carved teakwood desk. An oil painting of a tiger with two crossed scimitars hung on the wall behind the desk. *Kaplan* meant "tiger" in Turkish. The painting was the family coat of arms.

"Assassinating those government agents was a rash action, Major," Kaplan stated. "One we may all have reason to regret.''

"Do you regret doing business with the Kremlin?" Borgneff inquired stiffly. "I seem to recall that you had no qualms about taking certain risks when you learned we would pay you over a billion lira for your role in this operation.''

"I never concealed my motives, Major," the Turk answered mildly. "My only concern is my family. I have no loyalty to country or politics. Only my family matters. The rest of the world is a hostile battleground. I trust no one except my own blood.''

"You can trust us, efendi," Borgneff assured him. "The Soviet Union keeps its word. We are not like those capitalist scum who would betray you...."

"The KGB acts in its own interest," Kaplan declared. "Your organization manipulates, cheats, lies and kills to get what it wants."

"The KGB is fighting Western imperialism..." the Russian began.

"Save that nonsense for the dolts who believe in such foolishness," Kaplan snapped. "I do not criticize the methods of the KGB. They are, after all, identical to my own. Do not ask for trust, Major. I understand your organization. If I did not think we could work together successfully, I would not have agreed to our partnership. Just remember, in this country my power and influence is greater than your network of cowardly spies and lunatic terrorists."

"There is no need to make threats," the Russian sputtered as he frowned.

"I make no threats," Kaplan said simply. "I am reminding you of certain realities. *Evet?*"

"I won't forget," Borgneff assured him.

"My sons are waiting to discuss the next phase of our operation," Kaplan remarked. "I suggest you locate your comrades Kosnov and Suvarov. Then we shall all meet at the conference table. Just like your politicians in the Kremlin. I'm sure you'll enjoy that, Major."

Borgneff ignored the Turk's caustic remark and managed to smile at Kaplan. He wondered if he would ever see Mother Russia again.

7

The Sandalye Furniture Factory was located in the Harbiye area near Cumhuriyet Caddesi. It was a drab building with dirty windows and crumbling, gray stone. It was the sort of ugly little place no one would want to take a second glance at. An ideal choice for a terrorist safe house.

Calvin James, Rafael Encizo and Karl Hahn silently crept through an alley on the west side of the factory. They were dressed in camouflage black and armed for a soft probe that might suddenly turn hard. Each man carried a silencer-equipped machine pistol, as well as his personal side arm and other weapons.

"If we get caught we won't just walk out of an Istanbul police station again," Hahn whispered. "Do you know what Turkish prisons are like?"

"I saw *Midnight Express*," James muttered. "Sure hope they give the inmates orthopedic shoes...."

"*I* hope any terrorists inside are deaf," Encizo rasped. "Talk later."

I just hope we don't break into the place and find nothing but a group of frightened, scrawny refugees, Hahn thought. Encizo moved to the front door and quickly checked for evidence of alarm wires and booby traps. So far they had not found any alarms or other security devices guarding the factory.

Katzenelenbogen, McCarter and Manning were positioned at the opposite side of the building. They waited for the first team to enter via the main door. Encizo extracted a leather packet from his jacket and knelt by the door.

The Cuban took two slender lock picks from the kit and carefully inserted them into the keyhole. He worked the probes slowly until he felt the lock shift. A dull *click* rewarded his efforts. Encizo looked up at his partners and nodded to let them know he had unlocked the door.

Encizo unslung his Walther MPL submachine gun and held an index finger at the trigger. James readied his M-11 Ingram. The "little brother" of the M-10, the compact .380-caliber machine pistol was equipped with a 9-inch sound suppressor. Hahn had selected a Heckler & Koch MP-5A3, a favorite weapon of the West German border police, when he was a member of the GSG-9 antiterrorist unit.

The Cuban turned the knob. All three men stood clear of the door as Encizo slowly eased it open. The Cuban prepared to slip inside the building. Over the creaking of rusty hinges, Encizo heard a familiar *click-clack* from within the factory—the sound of a machine-gun bolt.

"Down!" the Cuban warned his partners.

The trio threw themselves to the ground as bullets ripped through the door, splintering wood, to sizzle above the heads of the prone commandos. The bellowing roar of a large-caliber machine gun bellowed from inside the factory like an angry dragon.

Calvin James rolled on his back and took an SAS concussion grenade from his belt. He pulled the pin and lobbed the explosive at the nearest window. Glass shattered as the grenade fell inside and erupted. Voices cried out as the "flash-bang" blaster violently shook the building.

Encizo slithered to the door and yanked it open with the front sight of his Walther subgun. The Cuban dived across the threshold, spraying the room with Parabellum slugs. He saw a lone figure twist in the shadows. The muzzle flash of the Walther illuminated the young Turkish terrorist. His chest was torn and bloodied by bullets as he fell against a wall and slumped to the floor.

The Cuban rolled to the cover of a large wooden desk. A terrorist lay crumpled in a corner next to the furniture. Apparently he had been hurled there by the force of the concussion grenade James had lobbed through the window. Encizo noticed three other men sprawled on the floor, stunned or dead after the explosion. One man moaned softly, but none moved.

Karl Hahn cautiously peered around the edge of the doorway and saw the bodies that littered the room. A Soviet-made DShK M1938 machine gun mounted on a tripod faced the front entrance.

Suddenly a shape appeared in the doorway opposite the entrance. An extended arm aimed a pistol at the German. Hahn triggered his H&K machine pistol first. The shape's head bounced. Blood splashed from its bullet-ruptured skull.

The terrorist collapsed, but another instantly took his place. A submachine gun snarled. Hahn retreated from the door as projectiles chewed into wood and plaster.

Although the gunman had seen Hahn, he was not aware of Encizo until the Cuban blasted him with the Walther MPL. A volley of 9mm slugs splattered the guy across the wall of a corridor beyond the office foyer.

Hahn entered quickly and joined Encizo. James prepared to follow, but a slight sound of wood sliding against wood arrested his attention. The black man glanced up in time to see a second-story window thrust open.

A bearded figure leaned out of the window and pointed a pistol at James. The Phoenix Force fighter snap-aimed his Ingram and fired a 3-round burst. The terrorist screamed as his face was shredded by .380 hollowpoint projectiles. He dropped his gun and tumbled over the edge of the windowsill to plunge to the ground below.

"The bastards are upstairs, too," James shouted. "Goddamn place is crawling with terrorists."

"Well," Encizo remarked as he shoved a fresh magazine into the Walther MPL, "that's what we came here for—isn't it?"

THE SHOOTING SIGNALED KATZ, McCarter and Manning that the soft probe had gone hard. It was time for Gary Manning to open a door for the trio. His method was less subtle than Encizo's, but just as effective.

The Canadian demolitions expert set a quarter pound of C-4 plastic explosives at the base of the large metal door leading to a truck bay at the rear of the factory. The Phoenix Force trio took cover behind some stacks of lumber. Manning triggered an electrical squib and detonated the C-4. The blast tore the metal door apart as if it were made of cardboard.

The effect was similar to kicking over an anthill. Half a dozen terrorist gunmen poured outside.

"Keep coming," David McCarter rasped, putting the wire stock of his Ingram to a shoulder. "We've got something for you."

The Briton leaned around the edge of a pile of wooden boards and thrust his M-10 at the charging terrorists. He opened fire, hosing the gunmen with Para-

bellum fury. Three Turkish fanatics were blasted off
their feet. Their bloodied bodies fell to earth as their
hate-rotted souls received a one-way ticket to hell.

A fourth terrorist tumbled across the pavement,
his right arm and shoulder smashed by bullets. The
other two dashed for the shelter of another pile of
lumber. They ran right into Katzenelenbogen's snarling
Uzi submachine gun. Full-auto 9mms cut the pair to
pieces.

The wounded gunman cursed under his breath as he
crawled toward the Skorpion machine pistol he had
dropped when bullets ripped his flesh and muscles. The
guy's left hand reached for the Czech blaster.

A boot suddenly struck the weapon, kicking the Skorpion beyond the man's groping fingers. The terrorist
stared up at David McCarter. Frightened and angry, the
Turk desperately tried to grab the Briton's ankle, hoping to throw McCarter off balance.

The English fighting machine did not cooperate. He
kicked the terrorist's arm aside and swiftly stamped the
edge of his boot into the man's throat, crushing his
windpipe.

Manning dashed to the ragged entrance of the bay. A
truck, parked inside, had been destroyed by the explosion. Chunks of metal and burning gasoline covered the
concrete floor. The Canadian took a deep breath and
charged into the flames.

He ran to the opposite side of the bay. Gasoline
splashed against his ankles. Manning jogged up a set of
stone steps to the loading platform. Heat seared his
flesh. The Canadian's right pant leg was laced with fire.

"Son of a bitch," he snarled, more annoyed than injured.

Manning quickly beat out the flames with his gloved

hands. A furious snarl drew his attention to a figure bolting forward from the shadows.

The terrorist wielded a wooden plank, four feet long and five inches thick. He swung the improvised club at Manning's skull. The Phoenix Force juggernaut blocked the club with his left forearm. The impact of the blow would have broken a less sturdy limb, but the Canadian was as tough as a lumberjack.

He countered with a powerful right cross to his opponent's jaw. The terrorist stumbled and fell into a wall. The man's jaw hung loosely on a broken hinge; blood oozed from his mouth. Yet he held on to the club and held it like a bar between his fists.

Manning shouted a *kiai* and swung a karate hammer-fist stroke to the plank. The board snapped in two. The startled terrorist found himself holding the broken halves in his hands, uncertain what to do next. Manning solved the problem by lashing a left hook to the guy's already-shattered jawbone. The Turk uttered an ugly gurgle as he fell to the pavement.

"Domuz!" a harsh voice growled.

Manning pivoted, his MP-5 held ready. Yet even as the Canadian moved, he knew he was too late. Automatic fire roared before he could trigger the pistol.

A husky Turk twisted in a macabre dance of death as he staggered across the floor. The terrorist dropped his machine pistol as another volley of bullets tore into his body and sent him sprawling across the concrete.

A shapeless form wrapped in a canvas tarp leaped up from the truck bay. Flames danced along the tarp as Yakov Katzenelenbogen rolled across the platform to smother the blaze. The Israeli discarded the charred shroud and quickly rose, his Uzi in his fist.

"Thanks, Katz," Manning said with a relieved sigh. "I owe you."

"Who keeps track?" Katz replied, gasping to get air into his smoke-filled lungs. "That fire is getting worse. McCarter will have to find another way inside."

"With a fight in progress, he'll find a way if he has to claw through a wall with his bare hands," the Canadian commented.

The thunderous rattle of full-auto weapons echoed from another position within the factory. Katz swapped magazines for his Uzi to be certain his weapon had a reliable supply of ammo.

"Sounds like our three friends at the front have found most of the action," the Israeli remarked. "Let's go see if they need any help."

8

Rafael Encizo, Calvin James and Karl Hahn had made certain there were no more terrorists lurking in the front office area before they moved to the assembly section of the furniture factory. This consisted of a large work area that comprised more than half the building.

It was also where most of the terrorists were stationed.

The two Phoenix Force veterans lobbed grenades into the assembly hall before they charged inside. James hurled another SAS concussion grenade, and the Cuban tossed a smoke canister. The combination of brain-rattling blast and blood-red billows of smoke confused and disoriented the terrorists.

The commando trio took advantage of the distraction to plunge into the hall. Encizo fired his Walther MPL as he ran to the cover of a metal conveyor belt. A terrorist leaped up from a cloud of crimson smoke, his arms shooting over his head as he executed an almost-graceful pirouette of death.

Encizo dropped to one knee by the pedestal of the conveyor. He trained the submachine gun on three ominous figures that moved through the red fog toward the Cuban's position. Encizo squeezed the trigger and watched a terrorist buckle and collapse as bullets punctured his torso. The Cuban swung his weapon toward the other two barbarians and squeezed the trigger again.

A feeble *click* was the only response.

"Mierda," Encizo rasped, discarding the empty sub-gun.

He chided himself for choosing the Walther MPL for the mission. The Walther fired full-auto only and thus tended to exhaust ammo much faster than an H&K, Ingram or Uzi. The Cuban did not have time to fret about this, as the two enemy gunmen were closing in fast.

Encizo dropped to a prone position. The terrorists' machine pistols erupted. Bullets rang angrily against the metal framework of the conveyor. The Cuban slithered to the gap beneath the assembly-line belt. He pulled the Smith & Wesson M-59 from its hip holster and snapped off the safety.

Encizo aimed the S&W autoloader at the advancing terrorists and opened fire. The Turkish goons were caught off guard by Encizo's counterattack from an unexpected position. The 9mm slugs sizzled into the terrorists' bellies. The Cuban took advantage of the 15-round capacity and double action of the M-59 to rapidly pump bullets into the pair. He finished off the Turks with two Parabellums in their skulls.

Calvin James had found shelter behind a concrete pillar. Two terrorists dashed right past his position without noticing the black man.

James aimed his M-11 at the unsuspecting Turks. He froze. Shooting men in the back, even terrorists who would not hesitate to murder innocent people in cold blood, repulsed James. Yet he could not allow the pair to get away.

"Are you assholes blind or just stupid, man?" he snapped in a loud, clear voice.

The pair whirled, surprise etched on their faces. James triggered the Ingram. Four .380 rounds burned a diagonal line across one man's chest. The second goon received a trio of hollowpoint slugs through the heart. James watched the pair wilt lifeless to the floor.

"Thanks," he muttered as he scanned the area for more terrorists.

He did not have to look very long to find some. An obese Turk and a wiry Oriental were headed toward James's position. The pair laid down a fan of fire as they advanced, but they had not spotted the black man's exact location, and none of the bullets came close. A voice screamed as several of the terrorists' stray rounds struck the wrong target.

"These turkeys are starting to kill one another," James whispered, aiming the Ingram at the pair.

He opened fire. The Oriental seemed to leap backward like a stunt man in a cheap kung-fu movie. The guy slammed into a wall and dropped to the floor like a bundle of blood-stained laundry.

However, the fat Turk roared with anger and charged ahead. He kept firing his Russian-made AKMS automatic rifle. Bullets pelted the pillar where James was stationed, but none struck flesh. The black man trained his M-11 on the Turk's chest and triggered another 3-round burst.

The brute kept coming. His bulky frame seemed to absorb the hail of bullets without feeling any pain. James elevated the Ingram and fired again. The Turk's head jerked. Twin jets of blood and brains squirted out the back of his skull. The Turk's body turned and finally crashed to the floor.

"Stay dead, damn it!" James snarled as he emptied the M-11 into the guy's twitching corpse to be sure he never got up.

Calvin reached for a fresh Ingram magazine. His hands trembled. James had been in combat many times before. Yet he had never seen a man keep coming with almost a dozen bullets in him before.

Get a hold of yourself, James thought, grateful that none of the other members of Phoenix Force could see him fumble with the Ingram to eject the spent magazine.

All of a sudden a figure rushed forward. James dropped the M-11 and reached for the .45 Colt Commander beneath his left arm. He cleared the holster, but a boot lashed out and kicked his forearm. The blow jarred his ulna nerve and the pistol fell from his suddenly numb fingers.

"Kara kopek!" his assailant spat with contempt.

The terrorist was a young Turk, slightly shorter than James but stocky and heavily muscled. A 9-inch blade jutted from his right fist. Tobacco-stained teeth appeared amid the killer's shaggy beard in a vicious smile of murderous victory.

James leaped away from a ruthless knife slash. The Turk was good. He immediately swung a backhand cut and followed with a quick thrust for James's belly.

The black warrior sidestepped from the path of the blade and jabbed his left fist into the terrorist's mouth. The Turk staggered back two steps. James pivoted and launched a spinning side kick into his opponent's abdomen. The terrorist groaned and fell to his knees.

The Turk was tough. He lashed a knife stroke at James's legs, hoping to cripple the black man. James jumped out of range. He pulled the G-96 Jet-Aer dagger from the sheath under his right arm.

"Come on, mother fucker," James taunted. "I'll show you how we do it back in Chi Town."

Calvin James was pissed off. He was angry with himself for being caught off guard. If the Turk had used a gun instead of a knife he would have killed the Phoenix fighter.

Long ago James learned that anger can make a man careless. In combat, this can get him killed. The commando knew how to control his anger, to channel his adrenaline to increase his strength and speed without affecting his reflexes.

The Turk rose to his feet. He still seemed confident of victory. The terrorist assumed a knife fighter's stance, the blade held low for deceptive slashes and thrusts. He struck out like a cobra, executing a fast lunge that suddenly became a wide belly slash.

James dodged the blade and swung a high sweep at his opponent's face. The terrorist instinctively raised his hands to protect himself. This was exactly what James had hoped he would do. The black man quickly snap-kicked the terrorist in the groin.

The Turk gasped and doubled up. Yet he desperately launched a knife thrust for James's ribs. The Phoenix pro caught the guy's wrist in his left hand and rapidly chopped the steel-capped butt of his G-96 to the top of his opponent's skull. The terrorist groaned and fell to his knees. James clipped him behind the ear with the knife butt and knocked the man unconscious.

Karl Hahn had also been busy staying alive. The German had located three terrorists behind a column of wooden crates piled four high. His eyes narrowed when he saw the trio. Hahn raised his pistol to his shoulder.

The German agent despised terrorists. He regarded them as mad dogs that walk on two legs instead of four. Hahn would not have hesitated to gun down all three of the Turkish fanatics if he had not recognized Hussein Ali Yazod among the trio.

He lowered the barrel of his machine pistol and opened fire. A salvo of 9mm slugs raked the legs of Yazod and one of the other terrorists. Shin bones snapped like crystal. The pair howled and tumbled to the floor.

The third gunman pointed a Skorpion at Hahn. The German's gun spat fire first. Bullets split the Turk's face. The terrorist died so fast he didn't even manage to scream before he fell.

Hahn switched the H&K pistol to his left hand and drew the Walther P-5 from his shoulder leather. He cautiously approached the two wounded fanatics. The pair groaned and clawed at their bullet-shattered legs. Yazod was the first to see Hahn. He still held a Stechkin machine pistol in his right fist. The terrorist raised his weapon.

Karl Hahn aimed his Walther carefully and squeezed the trigger. A Parabellum round drilled into the Iranian's elbow and burst the joint apart. Yazod shrieked and promptly fainted.

The last terrorist stared up at Hahn with utter dread as the BND agent drew closer. The Turkish zealot decided his only chance was to draw the Makarov pistol from his belt. This was the last mistake he would ever make. Hahn put a 9mm through the man's forehead.

Hahn heard the shuffle of shoe leather on concrete. He whirled, the H&K and Walther in his fists. A large wooden crate hurled toward the startled German. Hahn tried to dodge the giant projectile. He almost succeeded.

The edge of the crate struck Hahn's triceps, knocking the Walther from his grasp. The blow sent him stumbling across the room. The German collided with a workshop table. Saws, hammers and other tools rattled on the hooks of a wall rack. Hahn's left elbow slammed against a steel vise mounted on the table, and the blow jarred the MP5A3 from his fingers.

"Scheisser," Hahn rasped when he saw two terrorists close in for the kill.

The pair had hurled the crate at Hahn because they did not carry firearms. One terrorist wielded a large knife with a long, curved blade. His heavyset comrade was armed with a 3-foot-long iron crowbar.

The German glanced about, looking for something to use as an improvised weapon. He found a small cardboard box, full of metal tacks. Hahn scooped it up and hurled the contents at his opponents.

The terrorists cried out in alarm when the tacks pelted their faces. A nail head struck one man's left eyelid, but it didn't penetrate the skin. Two tacks hit the knife artist's mouth. He spat them out, blood dripping from a pricked lip.

Although neither aggressor had been injured by the tactic, it distracted them long enough for Hahn to take a wood saw from the wall rack. He held the tool like a cutlass short sword as the knife artist lunged forward.

Hahn chopped the saw blade at his opponent's wrist. Steel teeth sliced flesh. The terrorist cursed as the knife slipped from his grasp. Hahn suddenly closed in and pivoted sharply. He held the handle of the saw in one fist, while his other hand reinforced the blade.

Sharp metal struck the side of the terrorist's neck. Hahn's circular motion drew the saw teeth across the man's throat, cutting flesh and arteries. Blood spurted over the German's shirtfront as the Turk fell backward, both hands clamped to his slit throat.

Bellowing with rage, the crowbar-wielding terrorist delivered a murderous swing for Hahn's skull. The German dodged. Metal struck metal. The crowbar knocked the saw from Hahn's fist. The terrorist smiled cruelly and swung his weapon again.

Hahn leaped away from the flashing iron. His buttocks bumped the corner of the workshop table. The terrorist's crowbar descended in a vicious overhead stroke. Hahn sidestepped the attack, and the bar crashed into the table, splintering wood on impact. Hahn desperately grabbed a claw hammer from the tool rack.

The terrorist raised his crowbar again, but Hahn's hammer struck first. The steel head deflected the killer's weapon. Hahn quickly swung a backhand stroke. The claw blade of the hammer struck the terrorist's right temple. Metal split bone and pierced the Turk's brain. He dropped to the floor, the hammer lodged in his skull.

"You must have shocked the shit out of your shop teacher when you were a kid," James commented as he stared down at the bodies that surrounded Hahn.

The black man and Colonel Katzenelenbogen approached the German commando. Katz frowned when he recognized Hussein Yazod among the bloodied terrorists on the floor.

"Too bad you didn't manage to take him alive," the Israeli said with a sigh.

"Yazod isn't dead," Hahn replied. "But he will be if he doesn't receive medical treatment very soon."

"You guys are lucky I make house calls," James said, reaching for his medic kit.

9

Phoenix Force left the dead terrorists and most of the wounded for the Istanbul police to deal with. The authorities would haul in the survivors when they found the injured fanatics bound with riot cuffs and an arsenal on the premises—most manufactured in Communist countries. Dimitri Sandalye would also be held for questioning.

Manning, James and Hahn escorted Yazod and two other terrorists who survived the raid with a minimum of damage and loaded them into a truck Hahn had supplied for the occasion. The other members of Phoenix Force used fire extinguishers to put out the blaze in the truck bay. The gunshots and explosions would attract the police soon enough. There was no need for a fire, as well. Besides, the flames might destroy evidence or harm the men Phoenix Force left in the building.

Hahn drove the truck to a small warehouse near the Naval Museum along the coast of the Bogazici Strait. Ahmed, the mute, was waiting for them there. The big Turk met Phoenix Force at the door, a NATO G-3 assault rifle slung over his shoulder.

"I'll tell Ahmed to get rid of the truck," Hahn told the others. "Just in case someone saw us drive away from the factory."

"Good idea," Katz agreed, watching Manning carry Yazod into the warehouse. McCarter and Encizo herded the other prisoners inside at gunpoint.

"What method of interrogation shall we use?" Hahn inquired.

"Whatever works," the Israeli replied. "Threats, promises, truth serum, but no torture. Besides moral objection to such methods, torture is also too time-consuming. It can also be a waste of time when used on a true fanatic. The more you hurt them, the more they glory in suffering for the cause."

"I agree," the German assured him. "That's another reason to get Ahmed out of here. He tends to get impatient and believes direct action gets results faster."

"Yakov," Calvin James began as he approached the pair. "I checked out our prisoners. One guy's heartbeat is irregular and his blood pressure is pretty high. I think an injection of scopolamine would probably kill him."

"What about Yazod and the other terrorist?" Katz asked.

"The big dude with the blond beard has a ruptured eardrum," James answered. "But his heart is healthy enough. A dose of high-octane truth serum shouldn't do him any harm. I'm just not sure he'll be able to hear our questions well enough to answer them."

"And the Iranian?"

"He's shot up pretty bad," James answered. "I've given Yazod some morphine for the pain and I patched him up some, but those bullets will have to come out. We'll be lucky if he doesn't go into shock. Scopolamine is out of the question unless you want to execute him with the drug."

"Then we'll have to try something else," the Israeli mused. "Any ideas?"

"Sort of." The black man nodded. "It's a long shot and it might not work, but if I pump a little more morphine into Yazod he'll be feeling no pain at all. He'll be so relaxed he'll either be susceptible to suggestion or he'll simply pass out.''

'' 'Suggestion'?'' Hahn frowned. ''What sort of 'suggestion.' ''

''Hypnotic,'' James replied.

''Hypnotism?'' Hahn turned to Katz. ''Is he serious?''

''I'm serious, man,'' James snapped. ''I know it's a long shot, but it still might work.''

''I don't claim to know anything about hypnosis,'' the German began. ''But isn't it true a person won't do anything under hypnosis they wouldn't do if they were awake? So why would Yazod talk to us?''

''He wouldn't tell us shit,'' James agreed. ''*If* he knew who we really are. But he's going to be riding the Morphine Express. I'm hoping that will screw up his head bad enough so he won't know who he's talking to.''

''It's worth a try,'' Katz stated.

''I'll need some help,'' the black man told them. ''The questions should be asked in the subject's native language.''

''I speak a little Farsi,'' Hahn replied. ''But not enough for a detailed interrogation.''

''I speak Arabic,'' Katz declared. ''The language is very similar to Farsi.''

''It'll have to do,'' James said. ''Let's give it a shot and see if it works.''

Hussein Ali Yazod was moved to a small storage room to segregate him from the others. James carefully prepared another morphine injection and gave it to the injured terrorist. He waited for the drug to take effect. James checked the Iranian's heartbeat and peeled back an eyelid to examine the pupil.

''Okay, Katz,'' he began as he wrapped a cloth over the head of a flashlight. ''Yazod is ready.''

"What do we do now?" the Israeli asked.

"When I start talking to Yazod," the black man explained, "you translate everything I say into Arabic. Keep your voice low. Don't do anything to startle the dude. Okay?"

Katz nodded. James flicked off a wall switch to kill the ceiling light. Darkness filled the room. The black man sat in front of Yazod.

"Hussein," James said gently. "Relax, Hussein. Let all tension flow from your feet. The muscles are knotted, but now you can let them relax. Relax."

Katz found translating these instructions monotonous. James repeated them over and over. The black man told Yazod to relax his calves and his thigh muscles. Then his buttocks and lower back. Eventually James was telling the Iranian to relax the muscles in his face.

"You worked very hard today," James said. "You have accomplished much. All your work is done for now and you feel good about that. It was very hot today and you worked very hard. Now it is evening. The work is over. You can relax. It is no longer hot, and a cool sea breeze caresses your face as you enjoy a well-deserved rest."

Katz was tired of telling the terrorist to relax, but he continued to translate. Then James talked about a quiet, still pond and told Yazod to watch for the reflection of the moon on the water. The Israeli wondered if hypnosis was always such a boring business.

"Watch for the moon, Hussein," James repeated. "Watch for the moon."

He switched on the flashlight. The cloth subdued the glare to create a soft circle of light. James gradually moved the light as he described the moon creeping across the surface of the pond.

"Your eyelids are getting heavy," James instructed.

"Let them close. You can't keep your eyes open. Let them close and sleep. Sleep."

Katz opened his eyes. He shook his head to clear it. The Israeli translated James's instructions as the black man switched on a cassette tape recorder.

"Hussein," James said firmly. "Do you understand me?"

"Na'am," Yazod replied. "Yes."

"Do you know who I am?"

"Lah," the Iranian admitted. "No."

"I am the new cell leader of the People's Liberation Army," the black man declared.

"Where is Comrade Sandalye?" Yazod asked.

"He is at the base in Istanbul," James answered. "We have moved you to Ankara, where you will be safe."

"Amahn gayid," the Iranian replied. "It is good to be safe."

"Yes, Hussein," James confirmed. "But Sandalye and your other comrades in Istanbul are not safe. Istanbul is no longer safe. We have lost contact with them. Where is the Istanbul base so we can warn them."

"The base is at Sandalye's factory."

"The factory was destroyed by capitalist gangsters."

"I remember that now . . ." Yazod began.

"That is not important now," James insisted. "You are in Ankara. You are safe. Sandalye and the others who got away need your help. You must tell me where we can find them before the capitalists hunt them down first."

"I don't know where they would go," the Iranian replied. "I was never told about another base."

"Aw, shit," James muttered under his breath.

"But the Hungarian might know," Yazod stated.

" 'The Hungarian'?" James asked eagerly. "What Hungarian? Where do you find him?"

"He calls himself 'Noveny,'" Yazod explained. "He can be found at the Cekicbas Tavern on Milet Caddesi. It is said he spends the early afternoons there almost everyday."

"What is this Noveny?" James asked. "What does he do for us that makes him important?"

"He is connected with the drugs somehow," Yazod answered. "I'm not sure what he does. Helps to ship the heroin out of Turkey to Europe, I think."

"That's good, Hussein," James said sincerely. "Now, we need details about how progress has gone in Istanbul. Please tell us everything you remember about your activities and those of your comrades."

The other members of Phoenix Force questioned the other two prisoners. One terrorist refused to talk. McCarter and Encizo, experts at intimidation, threatened the guy. The Cuban showed him a few of the scars he received during torture by Castro's goons.

"They did this to me, *chico*," Encizo sneered. "So why should I mind doing the same to you?"

"You just supervise, mate." McCarter smiled. "I'll do it to him. After all, you got to do the last one."

The terrorist stubbornly refused to talk. He was surprised and relieved to discover the pair's threats were all bluff. Since the guy had a weak heart, they could not use scopolamine.

The blond terrorist was fit enough to receive the truth serum. The tawny-haired savage was a former member of the infamous Baader-Meinhoff gang. Hahn interrogated the German terrorist in his native tongue. The information acquired from him confirmed Yazod's story about the Hungarian go-between.

Phoenix Force had found their next lead.

10

Mustafa Kaplan liked to watch the *koylu*—laborers—in the poppy fields. He realized the men who worked the crop were not peasants. In fact, they were renegade Kurdish bandits who would have been tempted to cut a man's guts out for thinking of them as *koylu*.

Kaplan believed his family should still have peasants under their command. The Kaplan name had once been synonymous with "dynasty" among the agas of Turkey. Mustafa Kaplan's ancestors had been feudal lords during the reign of Emperor Constantine. When the Crusaders invaded Turkey in 1096, Kaplan warlords helped drive them back. A Kaplan warrior chief participated in the Goreme Valley battle, where Turks clashed with the dreaded Tafurs, who were despised even by other Europeans because they occasionally indulged in cannibalism.

The power of the Kaplan family and other agas in Turkey continued for centuries until the agrarian reforms became law. The agas struggled to retain their influence. Their efforts helped divide Turkey and nearly caused a civil war in the late 1950s.

Three military coups and four elections later, the landowners had little influence in the Turkish government. Kaplan was bitter and angry about this fall from power. Much of his property had been turned over to former peasants to use as independent farmland. The *koylu* had been his property. Giving the land to the *koylu* was like giving his land to sheep or goats. Such foolishness.

What right did the government have to steal his property or deny the Kaplan family the traditional power and prestige that had been part of their heritage. His ancestors had fought invading armies to hold their position of authority. They had spilled blood on the battlefield. All to have the land taken by those bastards in Ankara.

Thus Kaplan had decided to create a new dynasty. A shadow empire that forced him to deal with criminals, terrorists and the Soviet KGB. Kaplan did not question the morality of this scheme. He did not care if everyone in Western Europe became addicted to heroin or if the Russians conquered the entire world.

The Communists could do as they pleased as long as they granted the Kaplan family a position of authority in the new world order. Mustafa Kaplan's family was his nationality, politics and religion.

"Father," a voice called from the knoll beyond the poppy field.

Kaplan turned to see his eldest son, Erkut, approach. Tall and lean, Erkut resembled his father more than the other three offspring. Kaplan was very proud of all his sons, but Erkut was his favorite.

Erkut Kaplan had prepared well for the challenging ordeal his family had undertaken. Like his father, he felt loyalty only to kin. All efforts in life were directed toward reclaiming glory for the Kaplan family. Erkut had trained all his life for this goal.

His father had taught him the importance of keeping a still tongue around nonfamily members. Erkut had learned to control his emotions, especially anger and fear. He knew how to command men and how to deal with enemies.

Erkut had also acquired certain personal skills. He was an expert marksman with both rifle and pistol. Erkut had even learned how to pilot a helicopter. Mobility was necessary to maintain influence over others.

"Yes, Erkut," Kaplan greeted him. "Is something wrong, my son?"

"A message came on the radio in the helicopter, father," Erkut explained. "The Russian, Borgneff, says he must speak with you immediately. Something has happened that he feels is most important."

"The pig is probably out of vodka," Kaplan muttered with contempt. "Very well, Erkut. Shall we see what troubles our guest?"

Erkut flew the helicopter back to the Kaplan estate. Once a place fit for a sultan, the estate was still impressive. Stone walls surrounded the castle within. The minarets were used to call faithful Muslims to prayer. Actually, few of the residents at the estate claimed to be Muslims. Most were atheists. The minarets also served as watchtowers for sentries after nightfall.

A large parade field was located in the center of the estate. Once it had been a garden, but Kaplan had removed the flowers and covered the area with concrete and asphalt to serve a more practical purpose. The surrounding buildings were centuries old. Ornate, yet solid iron bars were built into most of the windows.

Erkut landed the helicopter on the parade field. Haukal, Kaplan's youngest son, met them as they emerged from the chopper. Haukal was slightly shorter but more muscular than Erkut. He had a unique ability to gain the trust and respect of the Kurdish renegades employed by Kaplan.

This was no small feat, since the Turks and the Kurds have been on very bad terms for over a century. The Turks had chosen to ignore the Kurds and refused to acknowledge Kurdish claims to territories in the mountain regions of the northeast. However, both the Kurdish bandits and the Kaplan family were renegades and thus formed a union based on mutual contempt for the rest of the world.

Haukal spoke the Kurdish tongue fluently and observed their tribal customs while in the presence of the bandit chief, Mavi-Ayi Bey. Young Kaplan had earned their respect by his skill as a horseman, rifle marksman and knife fighter. Haukal's success with the Kurds made him a very valuable asset to the family.

"Borgneff and the other Russian swine are waiting in the conference room," Haukal explained. "He's whimpering like an old woman because a terrorist base in Istanbul was apparently raided by some sort of commando strike force last night."

"The KGB is accustomed to intrigue," the senior Kaplan noted with a sigh. "But they have no stomach for battle. I think Borgneff should have stayed in Moscow. He is not strong enough to handle his mission here."

"Odd," Erkut remarked. "You criticized Borgneff for being too rash when he killed those two agents in Istanbul. Yet now he seems too timid."

"Most men are a paradox," Kaplan declared. "Do not expect them to be consistent, my son. A man may be brave one day and a coward the next. Sometimes he may be wise. Sometimes he may be a fool. But we have not heard all the facts yet. Perhaps the Russian has good reason to be concerned. We shall talk to him and find out."

A few minutes later, Kaplan met with Borgneff at the conference table in the Turk's version of a war room. Kaplan's other two sons, Bedri and Ali, were waiting for the rest of the family to arrive.

Bedri had been blessed with a handsome, lean face and a shrewd, keen mind. He had graduated from the Academy of Law in Ankara. Bedri could have had a fine career as a lawyer, but like his brothers, Bedri's loyalty to the family motivated his entire life. He served only one client and worked only for the sake of the Kaplan clan.

Ali was not as clever as his brothers, but he was physically the most powerful man in the room. Ali was built like a young ox. He could tear most men apart with his bare hands. However, Ali had a short temper and little self-control. Thus, he usually assisted one of the other brothers when additional muscle power was needed. Although he had no special talents to contribute to the family, Ali was totally dedicated to his father and brothers.

Borgneff's two KGB assistants were also present. Unlike the Hollywood stereotype, most Russian agents were not heavy-handed brutes with beetle brows and shifty pig eyes. Josef Ilyich Kosnov was a short, thin man who observed the world through the thick lenses of his steel-rimmed glasses. Kosnov resembled a file clerk more than a master spy. In fact, he generally worked as a clerk at the Soviet embassy in Ankara. This cover allowed him to spy on other personnel at the embassy.

Boris Ivanovich Suvarov's moon face and bright blue eyes created an innocent mask, but Suvarov was a cunning KGB operative. He specialized in exploiting political extremists and encouraging them to become terrorists—pawns of the KGB.

Kaplan felt contempt for the three Soviet agents. Russia had long been a traditional enemy of Turkey. War between the two countries had occurred in 1856 after Czar Nicholas I had demanded authority over the millions of Orthodox Christians living in Turkish territories. Turkey and Russia hadn't been on good terms since.

Kaplan chided himself for such notions. His family was his nation, not Turkey. For now, the KGB agents were his partners.

Borgneff told the rest that the Sandalye Furniture Factory had been attacked. "Whoever raided the base was not working with the National Security Service or the Istanbul police," the KGB operative concluded. "But whoever did it is very good. Very professional."

"How can you be sure of this?" Bedri Kaplan inquired. "Perhaps the NSS suspects your informers and they are feeding false information to these spies."

"My agent inside the NSS hasn't fallen under suspicion," Borgneff insisted. "I'm certain of that."

"That base was merely a hiding place for some terrorists." The senior Kaplan shrugged. "I fail to see that raiding such a place is very important to us. How much can the authorities learn from such rabble?"

"That is not the point, efendi," Borgneff said. "What matters is that someone has taken an interest in our operation. Whoever this mysterious enemy is, our contacts with Turkish intelligence and the American CIA haven't been able to find anything about them."

"International espionage is your field, Major," Kaplan stated. "Must I remind you that the British have agents in Turkey?"

"The English would not dare to act so boldly in a foreign land," Haubal said fiercely. "They are a paper lion that can only roar, but cannot claw or bite."

"Never underestimate the other side," Borgneff warned. "Especially the British or the Americans. They believe in playing by the rules, but there are no rules in espionage. The British learned this the hard way when MI6 was crippled by three KGB double agents who had managed to achieve high positions of power within that organization."

"That only proves how foolish the English are," Haubal snickered with contempt.

"But the British learned from that mistake," Borgneff told him. "The KGB will never have a high-ranking mole in British Intelligence again. The English also retaliated. I can't give you all the nasty details, but a lot of people in the Kremlin wish we'd never planted those moles."

"Then you agree that the British could be responsible?" Kaplan inquired.

"Perhaps," the KGB man said with a nod. "We're still trying to find out more about the incident."

"Then do it," Kaplan said simply. "Security is your responsibility."

"I know my job, efendi," the Russian snapped. "We're using every method possible to find out who these people are. We're also trying to predict what action they might take next. We'll be ready for them if they try anything."

"That is not good enough," Kaplan declared stiffly. "The next heroin shipment is due to leave in three days. If we can't afford to wait that long, I'll inform Captain Deniz to load his vessel and prepare to set sail tonight."

"But our people in France are not ready to receive the goods. . . ." Borgneff began.

"Then I suggest you see to it they are ready by the time Deniz arrives," Kaplan replied with a cold, hard smile.

11

Istanbul is actually two cities—European and Asian. Officially the two are divided by the Bosporus. However, the cultures have blended and geographical barriers mean little in Istanbul.

In the Old Town in the European section, one can buy Oriental rugs and enjoy *kebabci* and yogurt. In the Asian section one can go yachting at Salacak Beach or dine in restaurants that serve American and French cuisine. Christian churches, Jewish synagogues and Islamic mosques are found throughout the city.

Religion and culture have not always enjoyed such harmony in Turkey. Both Christian and Muslim rulers once forced their faith on their subjects. Much blood has been shed in Turkey over disputes about religion and cultural traditions. Tyrants and occupational governments ruled until the Turkish Republic was established in 1923 and Kemal Ataturk was elected president.

Kemal is regarded by many historians as one of the greatest men of the twentieth century. A strong and wise leader, Kemal was responsible for most of the reforms that helped stabilize Turkey and made the country a genuine nation.

However, blending cultures can produce some strange hybrids. The Cekicbas Tavern was such a social mutant. A *lokanta*—tavern—located on Milet Caddesi, the Cekicbas looked as if the first story had been designed by

Asian architects, while Europeans had built the second floor.

The front door and first story windows were tear-shaped spandrels associated with Islamic styles. The second story featured a balcony and French doors. The roof had a tile sheathing and slanted rafter common to European design. The Cekicbas may have been an oddity anywhere else in the world, but it did not look out of place in Istanbul.

Yakov Katzenelenbogen and David McCarter examined the tavern from the windows of a Citroën parked at the curb. Emlet sat behind the steering wheel. Ahmed, the mute, gazed out the windshield, watching the streets like a hungry falcon in search of prey.

"I hope Noveny is in there," McCarter remarked as he glanced at his black-faced wristwatch. "It isn't even noon yet."

"According to Yazod," Katz replied, "Noveny usually meets his contacts early in the day. There is a certain logic in that. One doesn't generally think of sinister characters conducting illegal business in a public place in broad daylight."

"Still seems a bit risky for KGB," the Briton said. "I can't imagine any of the perfumed uncles doing business this way."

The term "perfumed uncles" was a slang expression for a KGB overseer who coordinated intelligence operations in foreign countries. The expression was started by Czechoslovakian intel officers who were amused by the habit of many Russian case officers of dousing themselves with perfume. Such Communist extremists proudly claimed they had to do this because their devotion to the Party did not leave them enough time to bathe.

"I doubt that Noveny is KGB," Katz agreed. "Probably a Hungarian agent being used by the Russians to avoid a direct Soviet link with the heroin trade. He's still the best target we've found so far.''

"Then let's go have a chat with the bloke,'' McCarter said, smiling like a shark that smelled blood.

The Phoenix Force pair emerged from the French Citroën. Dressed in a lightweight suit and a gray fedora, Katz looked more like a European merchant than a commando. He wore a pair of pearl-gray gloves. The prosthetic device at the end of his right arm appeared quite lifelike, until one noticed that the five "fingers" were unusually rigid.

McCarter's tan suit was wrinkled and his houndstooth tie had been loosened at the throat. The Briton had never been a dapper dresser, but he looked like a harmless tourist. McCarter's jacket hung loosely on his lean frame. It concealed the telltale bulge of the Browning Hi-Power holstered under his left arm.

Katz and McCarter walked to the Cekicbas Tavern and pushed through a beaded curtain to enter the *lokanta*. A fat, bearded bartender leaned against the counter. He barely glanced up from a newspaper that lay open on the bar. Four men sat at a table amid a gray mist of cigarette smoke. Katz approached the bar.

""*Bonjour, monsieur,*'' he said to the bartender. "*Parlez-vous français?*''

"Yes,'' the man replied wearily. "I speak French. What do you want to drink, monsieur?''

The Israeli placed two ten-lira bills on the counter. The bartender looked down at the money and licked his lips.

"We would like some information,'' Katz explained. "Where can we find a Hungarian who calls himself 'Noveny'?''

"That information will cost you one hundred lira, monsieur,'' the fat man declared.

Katz nodded and gave him eighty more lira. The bartender gathered up the money and stuffed it into his pockets.

"Noveny is over there," he said. "At the only table where anyone is seated."

"You're a shrewd businessman, monsieur," McCarter said, a razor's edge to his voice. "Noveny had better be at that table. We can be most unpleasant to anyone who tries to cheat us."

"What do you mean by that?" the bartender demanded.

"You'd better hope to God you never find out," the Briton replied with an icy smile.

McCarter and Katz headed toward the four men at the table. Three of them immediately rose from their chairs. The trio were built like concrete slabs, with black ice for eyeballs. They happened to be Turks, but their breed would have been labeled "hoodlum" regardless of race or nationality.

"We want to talk to Monsieur Noveny," Katz stated.

The Israeli ignored the three muscle boys and stared directly at the man who was still seated. He figured the guy was in charge, and that meant he was probably Noveny. The Hungarian was a short, paunchy man with a trim mustache and a rubbery mouth. Dark glasses covered his eyes, but two bushy brows were raised above the rims of the lenses.

"What do you want with him, monsieur?" Noveny inquired, his French containing a thick Slavic accent.

"We're not accustomed to discussing business with an audience," McCarter stated, jerking his head toward one of the Turkish thugs.

"These gentlemen are my business associates," Noveny explained. "They stay with me, or we don't talk."

"If you feel insecure," Katz began, "have them wait at another table where they'll be close enough to come to your rescue if you feel that is necessary."

"No one dictates terms to me," Noveny told him. "Accept my conditions or get out of here."

"Very well," Katz agreed with a shrug. "We accept your conditions—providing they remain reasonable, of course."

"Abdul," Noveny snapped at the bartender. He uttered a rapid command in curt Turkish.

"Evet, efendi," the bartender replied quickly, bobbing his head as if trying to work it loose from his neck.

Abdul hurried to the front entrance. He slammed shut a thick wooden door and bolted it. Katz and McCarter felt the familiar rush of adrenaline pulsate through their veins. The sixth sense of a combat veteran warned them that the situation was about to get very hot very fast.

"Now that our privacy is assured," Noveny began, interlacing pudgy fingers on his round belly, "my associates will frisk you both. Sorry, but I must insist."

"We understand," Katz assured him as he raised his arms.

McCarter followed his partner's example and raised his hands. Two of the hoods approached. Katz shrugged helplessly.

"No need to touch me up," he said, sighing, "there is a gun in a shoulder holster under my right arm."

One of the goons smiled and reached under Katz's jacket for the pistol. The Israeli seemed to explode in his face.

Katz suddenly slammed the heel of his left palm into the Turk's forearm. The startled thug's arm was knocked aside. Katz's right arm flashed. He chopped the edge of his steel "hand" between his opponent's eyes, cracking the glabella on impact. The man was dead before he hit the floor.

"Nem!" Noveny cried out as he watched his bodyguard collapse.

The Hungarian awkwardly tried to rise from his chair. Katz kicked the table, driving it into Noveny's chest. Man and furniture crashed to the floor. The Israeli whirled, drawing his SIG-Sauer P-226 automatic in a single, swift motion.

The bartender suddenly found himself staring into the muzzle of Katz's pistol. Abdul's arms instantly shot overhead in surrender. Katz did not worry about Noveny's other two goons, confident McCarter would take care of them.

The Briton did not disappoint him. The two Turkish muscle boys had been surprised and distracted by Katz's unexpected actions. McCarter took advantage of this and quickly seized the closest man before the hood could reach for a weapon.

McCarter expertly nutted the Turk, butting his forehead into the bridge of the guy's nose. The Englishman rammed a knee between the man's splayed legs and followed up with a solid right cross to the thug's face.

The Briton shoved his dazed opponent into the third henchman. He swung an uppercut to his first adversary's jaw. The man's knees buckled, and he slumped unconscious at McCarter's feet. The English commando instantly attacked the other muscle boy.

He swung his left fist at the Turk, but the thug blocked the punch with a forearm. The goon countered with a left hook. McCarter parried the attacking arm with his right palm.

The Phoenix Force pro's shoulders turned sharply as

he shoved the Turk's arms to cross each other. The thug's forearms were tangled together for a second, which was long enough for McCarter to smash the front of his right elbow against the side of his opponent's skull.

McCarter snapped a back fist to the Turk's face. The guy's head bounced back, exposing his throat. The Briton lashed a light karate chop to the Turk's windpipe. The hoodlum crumpled in a choking heap. McCarter kicked him behind the ear to make certain he did not get up for a while.

"So much for subtlety," Katz said dryly, still pointing his SIG-Sauer at Abdul.

"This way was more fun, anyway," McCarter commented, drawing his Browning to cover the Hungarian.

"You're not Turks," Noveny declared as he rose and dusted himself off. "What are you? Interpol? American CIA? My lawyer will still rake you both over the coals for this. Your own embassy will see to it you go to jail."

"We don't have an embassy, Noveny," Katz told him. "And your lawyer won't help you."

McCarter and Katz bound the Hungarian's wrists behind his back and did the same for Abdul. The Israeli chopped the side of his hand into Abdul's neck muscle to render the fat man unconscious.

"Who are you?" Noveny insisted.

"For chaps like you," McCarter began as he shoved the Hungarian toward the door, "we can be a bloody nightmare."

12

Katz and McCarter escorted Noveny outside and pushed him into the Citroën. McCarter joined the Hungarian in the back seat, while Katz slid into the front next to Ahmed. The big Turk smiled and nodded his approval.

Ahmed started the engine. The Citroën pulled away from the curb and started south on Milet Caddesi. A green Volkswagen Beetle emerged from an alley and followed the French car.

"Looks like we've picked up a tail already," McCarter commented as he glanced out the rear window. "Figured that would happen."

"I'm glad you weren't disappointed," Katz said dryly. "Hand me the walkie-talkie."

"Here you go, mate," the Briton replied, giving Katz the transceiver.

Yakov switched on the radio. "This is Escort calling Hawk One, Two and Three. Do you read me? Over."

"Hawk One," Calvin James's voice replied. "Read you fine. Over."

The black warrior was seated on a BSA motorcycle, riding along Ataturk Boulevard. The wooden stock of a short-barreled weapon jutted from a scabbard attached to the chopper. James's leather jacket was open to allow him to draw his Colt Commander if he needed it in a hurry.

"Hawk Two," Rafael Encizo's voice called next. "Read you, Escort. Over."

The Cuban rode in a Saab driven by Karl Hahn. The German drove the combat import toward Escort's position on Milet Caddesi. Encizo and Hahn were well armed and ready for trouble.

"Three here," Gary Manning's voice announced from Katz's transceiver. "I've got a bird's-eye view. Is that a shadow, Escort? Over."

The Canadian had an excellent position on the roof of the Roman aqueduct on Ataturk Boulevard. He could see most of Istanbul from his perch, thanks to a pair of Bushnell Armored 8 x 30 binoculars.

"I trust everyone heard that," Katz spoke into the mouthpiece of his walkie-talkie. "So you all know what to do. Watch yourselves. There's bound to be more than one shadow around. Over."

"Affirmative, Escort," Manning assured him. "Over."

"We'll take care of everything," Encizo added. "Over."

"I sure as shit hope so," James's voice remarked. "Over."

"Good luck," Katz told his teammates. "Over and out."

The Citroën turned off Milet Caddesi onto Ataturk. The green Beetle continued to follow the Phoenix Force vehicle. A few cars crept along the boulevard. People on bicycles and mopeds comprised most of the traffic. Ahmed gradually increased speed.

"*Vorsichtig*, Ahmed," Katz told the driver, speaking German. "Careful. We don't want to harm any innocent bystanders. *Verstehen Sie*?"

Ahmed nodded in reply.

McCarter had gathered up a briefcase from the floor. He opened it and removed his M-10 Ingram machine pistol. A 32-round magazine was already inserted in the butt. The Briton worked the bolt to feed the first 9mm cartridge into the chamber and switched on the safety catch.

"Escort," Manning's voice called from the walkie-talkie. "Looks like another shadow up ahead. Over."

"Are you sure?" Katz asked. "Over."

"Looks like a possible ambush," Manning replied.

"I see it," James's voice cut in. "On my way. Over."

The black fighting machine had spotted the second enemy vehicle. A dark-brown Datsun had emerged from an alley and pulled onto Ataturk Boulevard. The car parked by a curb and three men climbed out.

They made no effort to hide their intentions. Their faces were covered by the scarfs of their kaffiyehs. The terrorists waved Russian-made AK-47 automatic rifles. Frightened pedestrians bolted in all directions.

Men and women cried out in alarm. A panicked taxi driver stomped on the gas pedal when he saw the masked gunmen. The cab streaked forward and swung into another lane, nearly striking Calvin James. The black man steered his chopper away from the charging vehicle and continued to speed toward the terrorists.

James reached for the scabbard and drew a weapon that resembled a sawed-off shotgun with an enormous barrel. He drove the BSA past the terrorists' position. The gunmen barely glanced at the cyclist, assuming he was fleeing from them like the other passersby.

One of the terrorists noticed James held something that looked like a large piece of pipe, but he saw only a blur and could not identify the object.

The motorcycle hopped onto a sidewalk and narrowly avoided a cartful of *simits* and other pastries that had been abandoned by the vendor. The black commando came to an abrupt halt and leaped from the BSA. He lost his balance, fell, rolled and rose to one knee. The M-79 grenade launcher was still in his fists.

James aimed it at the terrorists' position and pulled the trigger. A 40mm grenade hurtled directly into the side of the gunmen's Datsun. The heavy explosive charge blasted the car apart like a crystal goblet hurled against a stone fireplace.

Shards of glass and metal filled the sky. The terrorist trio were thrown ten violent feet by the explosion. Their mutilated, dismembered bodies were very, very dead.

The Citroën arrived a few seconds later. The wreckage of the enemy Datsun littered the road. A pool of burning gasoline crept along the gutter. Ahmed clenched his teeth and drove past the wreck.

Katz and McCarter saw Calvin James wave his M-79 in a victorious salute before he mounted the BSA motorcycle once more.

The green Volkswagen still chased the Citroën along the boulevard. The driver saw the burning remnants of the Datsun and responded by bolting past the scene, fearful of facing a similar fate. Yet the VW did not break off its pursuit.

"Hawk One to Hawk Two and Three," James spoke into his walkie-talkie. "Shadow Two is dust in the wind, but Shadow One is still on Escort's ass. Didn't want to blow it up just in case it isn't full of bad guys. After all, nobody in the VW has started shooting yet. Over."

"Next time shoot at the tires, Hawk One," Encizo's voice replied curtly.

"That would make a speeding vehicle go out of control, Hawk Two," Katz cut in sharply. "Hawk One did the right thing. A couple of right things. Good work. Over."

"Thanks, Escort," James said happily. "I'm about to tag after the VW...."

"No," Katz insisted. "Break off pursuit, Hawk One. You're too easy a target. Too vulnerable on that cycle. Over."

"Hawk Two to Escort," Hahn's voice announced. "We're coming up fast. Will follow the VW. I suggest Hawk One pull onto Vatan Caddesi and make a right on Haziran. That will lead to the aqueduct without exposing him to enemy fire. Over."

"Thanks for directions, Hawk Two," James replied. "Over."

The German and Encizo were gaining on the enemy Beetle. Hahn knew the streets of Istanbul as well as he knew those of Nuremberg or Munich. He had no trouble keeping up with the terrorist vehicle as he drove the Saab along Ataturk. Encizo worked the bolt of a Heckler & Koch MP-5A3.

"I still think we should shoot out their tires," he muttered. "Or is that too corny?"

"If it works," Hahn replied, never taking his eyes from the windshield, "who cares if it's corny? But maybe we can just run them off the road, providing we can find a place that won't cause a wreck."

"Try that and I bet they'll start shooting at *us*," Encizo commented.

"And we could shoot back," the German stated simply.

"You're right." Encizo grinned. "Let's run 'em off the road and end the suspense...."

The unexpected rattle of high-velocity projectiles striking the metal skin of the Saab startled the pair. A spiderweb pattern appeared in the rear window as bullets struck reinforced glass.

"Hawk Two," Manning's voice called from the walkie-talkie next to Encizo. "Enemy vehicle behind you."

"We noticed," the Cuban rasped into the radio.

"Keep your heads down and keep moving for the aqueduct," the Canadian advised. "I'll take care of the bastards."

"Okay, Hawk Three," Encizo agreed. He switched off the radio. "Where are all those fancy James Bond gadgets when you need them?"

"In the movies," Hahn said, his voice strained from the tension. "We're getting close to the aqueduct. Hang on, my friend."

"Do I have a choice?" the Cuban replied.

Gary Manning was still stationed on the summit of the Aqueduct of Valens, viewing the streets below through his field glasses. He had been able to observe the car chase from the best vantage point. Now the caravan was coming closer. One way or the other, it would all be over in a few more minutes.

The Citroën with Katz, McCarter, Ahmed and Noveny reached the aqueduct first. It sped across the cobblestone road and through one of the aqueduct's archways. The green Beetle followed. Hahn and Encizo in the Saab appeared next. They were being pursued by a battleship-gray Citroën. A hooded terrorist leaned out a window and fired a machine pistol at the Saab.

"How theatric," Manning muttered as he raised an FLN assault rifle to his shoulder and peered through the telescopic sight mounted on the steel frame.

He tracked the gray car until the cross hairs divided the face of the terrorist behind the steering wheel.

The Canadian marksman squeezed the trigger. A 7.62mm armor-piercing projectile punched through the windshield of the enemy Citroën. The driver convulsed behind the wheel, throwing the car into a screaming skid across Ataturk Boulevard.

The idiot terrorist who had been hanging out the window was thrown from the vehicle. His body bounced off the cobblestones and smacked head first into a lamppost. His skull split open like a ripe melon, spilling brains on the sidewalk.

Hahn drove the Saab through an arch and continued to follow the first two cars. The gray Citroën whirled out of control and crashed lengthwise into one of the Roman columns supporting the aqueduct. A figure was chucked through the windshield. If the terrorist had not been dead when he burst from the glass, he certainly was by the time his body quit tumbling across the pavement.

Ahmed drove onto Akeiger Caddesi and headed for a construction site. Workers scrambled from the area. They had heard the gunshots and explosions. Anyone in Istanbul over the age of five recalled the terrorist epidemic of the 1970s. A wise civilian knew when to run for cover.

Construction workers on the steel girders of the skeletal frame of a building stared down in astonishment as the Phoenix Force vehicle roared onto the scene. The car swerved behind a bulldozer and came to a dead stop.

David McCarter and Yakov Katzenelenbogen leaped from the Citroën. The Briton moved to the great steel shovel of the dozer, his Ingram in both fists. Katz had left his Uzi in the trunk of the car, so he had to rely on the P-226 pistol as he positioned himself behind the frame of the dozer.

The Volkswagen appeared. The driver saw the Citroën behind the bulldozer and immediately stomped on the brake. A terrorist armed with a NATO G-3 assault rifle emerged from the passenger side. McCarter rose up and fired a spray of 9mm slugs into the enemy gunman. The terrorist fell against the side of the VW and slid lifeless to the ground.

The driver of the Volkswagen turned the wheel desperately and stomped on the gas pedal as if it were a scorpion about to sting his ankle. The car swung a full circle and bolted into a hasty retreat, heading straight for Hahn's Saab. The German and Encizo had just arrived at the construction site.

The Cuban popped open a door and opened fire with the H&K machine pistol. A volley of Parabellum rounds dissolved the windshield of the Beetle. The enemy car turned sharply and nose-dived into a pile of red bricks. Metal crunched as the front end of the Volkswagen crumpled like a paper cup.

"All shadows are out of the game," Gary Manning's voice announced via the walkie-talkies of the other members of Phoenix Force. "But the Istanbul boys in blue are headed this way. There's half a dozen cop cars speeding down the boulevard. Better haul ass."

"Read you, Hawk Three," Katz spoke into his transceiver. "We'll meet at the safe house on Karakoy in twenty minutes. Over and out."

13

A superprofessional like Colonel Katzenelenbogen would never give the true location of a secret meeting place across a radio when someone might be listening on the same wavelength. He had mentioned Karakoy to throw off any unwanted trackers who may have tapped into their broadcast.

Phoenix Force had always planned their rendezvous point in advance. They abandoned the Citroën and the Saab near the Sulimaniye Mosque and mingled with a group of tourists. McCarter had cut the riot cuffs off Noveny's wrists and warned the Hungarian he would break his neck if the guy tried to call for help or flee.

They divided into pairs and took separate taxicabs to the majestic Topkapi Palace in the southeast peninsula of Eminonu. The palace was a favorite among sightseers. A truly awesome structure, it exhibited several different styles of architecture, including Roman, Ottoman and Islamic. The palace was actually a collection of buildings. From a distance, one building seemed to have twin tortoise shells on its roof. Another appeared to have a cluster of headstones on its summit.

However, Phoenix Force had not come to Turkey to see the sights or to stroll the gardens of the Topkapi Palace and smell the tulips. Karl Hahn had arranged for an old U.S. Army truck to be left in an alley near the palace in case they needed yet another vehicle for the mission.

"Who are you men?" a terrified Noveny asked as he sat in the back of the truck surrounded by Katz, Mc-Carter and Manning. "What do you want?"

"We want some answers," Katz replied as he pulled the glove from his right hand to reveal the steel prosthesis. The index finger was hollow. It was actually the barrel of a single-shot .22 Magnum pistol, built into the hand.

"I demand to call the Hungarian embassy," Noveny declared.

"Why don't you want to contact the Soviet embassy?" Gary Manning inquired, speaking French with a Quebec accent.

"I am a Hungarian national," Noveny told them. "You can check my passport if you don't believe me."

"No doubt you are a Hungarian," Katz remarked. "You're certainly not bright enough to be a KGB agent. The perfumed uncles from Moscow like to use greedy little morons like you. Why risk losing Russian agents when they can get a small-time gangster like you to do their dirty work for them."

"And you'll take the blame, Noveny," McCarter added. "You'll go to prison for espionage, conspiracy, drug smuggling and whatever else the Turks decide to charge you with."

"Don't tell him such lies," Katz snorted. "Noveny is stupid, but even he isn't stupid enough to believe we'll simply turn him over to the authorities. Not after we've kidnapped him and he witnessed that gun battle in beautiful downtown Istanbul."

"That's true." McCarter sighed. "Besides, we'd have too much trouble trying to explain why Noveny will be cut up a bit and decorated with a lot of cigarette burns and such."

"What do you mean?" the Hungarian stammered fearfully.

"We're going to make you very unhappy, Noveny," Gary Manning replied simply. "Unless you tell us about the KGB's heroin business."

"I can't tell you what I don't know. . . ." Noveny began.

"Like most Communists," Katz cut in, "you're unrealistic, Noveny. Let me explain some facts to you. The Russians won't protect you. You're expendable. Now that you've been captured, you're just an embarrassment. That means the KGB will kill you if they get the chance."

"I've got an idea," McCarter announced cheerfully. "Let's beat the hell out of Noveny. Break a couple of bones. Maybe pull out some teeth or toe nails with a pair of pliers. . . ."

"That sounds like a lot of fun," Manning remarked, playing along with McCarter. "But what if Noveny still doesn't talk?"

"Then we'll just drop him off at the Soviet embassy," McCarter said with a grin. "The KGB will be convinced he told us something. Just the fact that he's been connected with the Russians will get him in a lot of trouble with the KGB."

"That would be a cruel thing to do to Noveny." Katz frowned. "You're aware of what the KGB does to prisoners. Even Amnesty International has recorded dozens of incidents of torture at the Butyrka Prison in Moscow. The Kremlin still authorizes human experiments on political prisoners. I've heard some of those Siberian camps make Dachau look like a summer resort."

"You're right." The Canadian nodded. "It would be a terrible thing to do to Noveny."

"But we'll have no choice unless he decides to cooperate with us," Katz said with a shrug.

"How do I know you won't kill me if I talk?" the Hungarian demanded. "Not that I'm confessing to anything."

"Why would we want to kill a defector?" the Israeli asked, his eyebrows raised in mock surprise. "You're certainly worth more to the free world alive than dead if you agree to defect to the West."

"Defect?" Noveny frowned.

"What other choice do you have?" Manning inquired. "You can deal with us or the KGB."

"I don't want to be an American," Noveny snorted.

"America can get along without you," Katz assured him.

"So can England," McCarter added.

"I want to go to a country where I speak the language," Noveny decided. "I shall defect to the French Embassy in Ankara. Take me there."

"This isn't a ruddy taxicab, you bastard," McCarter growled. "And you can defect to the bloody Vatican for all we care, but you'll tell *us* about the KGB's heroin operation before you go anywhere."

"I don't know who is supplying the narcotics," Noveny answered. "But I can tell you how it is being smuggled out of Turkey."

"We don't need a dramatic pause, Noveny," Katz said sharply. "This isn't a screen test. Now where are the smugglers?"

"Find Captain Deniz," the Hungarian told them. "His ship is named the *Altinkaz*. You'll find it at a harbor along the Halic."

"The 'Halic'?" Manning frowned.

"Yes," Noveny confirmed. "Better known as the Golden Horn."

14

The Golden Horn was a colorful name for a rather drab and badly polluted waterway that flowed through Istanbul. The Halic received this romantic title centuries ago, although it was murky and muddy even before industrial wastes were dumped into the water.

According to legend, two ships bearing a fortune in gold were sunk in the Halic when Mehmet II conquered Constantinople in 1453 A.D. To this day, treasure hunters still dive into the Horn in search of the gold that supposedly lies somewhere on its muddy bottom.

Saat Harbor was a dirty little pier located south of the Ataturk Bridge. A small, shabby warehouse was the only structure in the immediate area. Most of the vessels on the Golden Horn were either ferries or garbage scows, but a cargo ship was docked at Saat Harbor.

The five men of Phoenix Force and Karl Hahn were crammed inside the back of a gray van parked a block away from the harbor. The vehicle was equipped with some pretty impressive special gear that included extra weapons, sound-amplification devices and an infrared periscope with the top lens disguised as an air vent on the roof.

"Madre," Rafael Encizo muttered as he gazed through the periscope. "That's a big ship for such a cruddy little pier."

"One wouldn't travel from Turkey to France in a tugboat,'' Katz commented, checking the foot-long sound suppressor attached to the barrel of his Uzi submachine gun.

''I don't understand why they take it all the way to Western Europe,'' Manning commented.

''Where else could they deliver the heroin?'' Hahn inquired as he chambered a round into his Walther P-5 and clicked on the safety. ''The easiest delivery route would be along the Black Sea to Bulgaria, but then the narcotics would require distribution by agents from a Communist satellite country of the Soviet Union. Everyone knows Moscow runs Bulgaria. If anyone discovered the Bulgarians were involved in narcotics, the Russians would immediately be labeled as the true culprits.''

''The shipment could be transported along the Aegean Sea to Greece,'' the Canadian suggested.

''The Greeks and the Turks don't get along very well,'' Hahn explained. ''The Greek authorities would be extremely suspicious of any Turkish vessel coming near the shores of Greece. The only way the Soviets can deliver the heroin to Western Europe without risking a direct link to their involvement in the scheme is by sending the drugs via the long route to France.''

''We've got to be certain the men on board that ship are smuggling heroin,'' Katz stated. ''Noveny may have lied to us.''

''I doubt that, Yakov,'' McCarter said. ''Too many things indicate this is the right place. Besides, Noveny was too scared to be a good liar, unless he's one bloody great actor.''

''Any good intelligence agent has to be a bloody great actor,'' the Israeli replied.

''That Hungarian lump of shit doesn't strike me as being an intel professional,'' McCarter insisted. ''He's just a goddamn puppet for the KGB. A go-between for the terrorists and the smugglers.''

"Probably true." Katz sighed. "But we can't just charge in there and start shooting people."

"I should hope not," Hahn said dryly. "You five will go home after this mission is over, but I'll be stationed in Turkey for another year."

"Will you return to Germany then?" Manning inquired.

"I've promised not to do a 'Charles Bronson' when I get back," Hahn said with a grin. "I won't be hunting down Red Army terrorists anymore. I just hope they give me something interesting in the future."

"You got any family in Germany?" James asked as he slid a magazine into the well of his Smith & Wesson M-76 subgun.

"That depends on what you call 'family,'" the German replied.

"Wife and kids?" the black man inquired.

"No children and just an ex-wife—thank God," Hahn declared with a groan. " 'Greta Garbage,' I call her. One good thing about my profession is it makes one difficult to find. I've been able to avoid alimony payments for nearly three years now. Maybe I should stay in Istanbul, after all."

"Let's have the bloody tea party later," McCarter said crossly. He was eager to get into the thick of whatever action awaited them.

"Heads up!" Encizo announced, still gazing through the periscope. "There's a lot of activity out there. Looks like they're loading something on board the *Altinkaz*. Sacks of grain—or at least that's what they're supposed to look like."

"They might be planning to leave tonight," Calvin James remarked.

"Then we have to act now," Katz declared. "But remember, we must make certain those people are the enemy."

"Okay," Encizo agreed. "There are two guys in front of the warehouse. Probably sentries. Let's see what we can learn from them."

"But if those dudes on board that ship are pushing shit," James said in a cold, hard voice, "we burn 'em."

"We know how you feel about drug dealers," Katz told him. "But don't forget, a corpse can't talk and we have to find the people who are really behind this heroin business."

"Don't worry," the black warrior assured him. "I won't lose my cool. Still, it isn't likely those turkeys will surrender without a fight."

"God, I hope not," McCarter said with a wry grin.

KARL HAHN AND RAFAEL ENCIZO walked toward the warehouse. Both men wore pea jackets, dark slacks and black wool caps. Their arms swung loosely at their sides, gloved hands empty. The two sentries stiffened when they saw Hahn and Encizo. One guard slipped a hand inside his coat. The other shoved both hands in the pockets of his camel's-hair coat.

"Merhaba," Hahn greeted them.

"Ne istiyorsunuz?" one of the sentries demanded gruffly, straining his eyes to try to see the strangers' faces in the dark.

"Kaptan Deniz, ariyorum," the German replied. "I want to see Captain Deniz."

"Who are you?" the guard demanded.

"Noveny sent us," Hahn answered.

"What does that Hungarian pig want?" the Turk snorted.

"He sent us to warn Deniz about the heroin shipment," Hahn said in a casual manner.

"What's wrong with the shipment..." the other guard began.

"Shut up, you idiot!" the first sentry snapped. "These two might be police."

"Relax," Hahn urged. "Just let us talk to the captain."

"After we've frisked you two," the sentry said as he drew a revolver from his jacket.

Suddenly the Turk yelped in pain as a hypo dart struck the side of his neck. The needle pierced skin and injected three hundred milligrams of thorazine into his bloodstream. The sentry staggered backward and blinked in surprise. Then he dropped his handgun and passed out.

The second guard cursed and pulled a compact automatic pistol from the pocket of his coat. He made his move too late. Encizo had already closed in. The Cuban caught the sentry's wrist and adroitly twisted the gun from his hand.

Hahn quickly moved behind the guard and seized the collar of the guy's camel hair. The German pulled forcibly and punted a foot into the back of the Turk's knee. The sentry's legs buckled and he fell to his knees. Encizo slammed a heel-of-the-palm stroke to the mastoid bone behind the man's right ear, and the guard slumped to the ground, unconscious.

David McCarter quickly approached. He held a Bio-Inoculator in his fist. A B-I pistol is a powerful dart gun that is usually used to tranquilize large animals. Gary Manning followed. He also carried a Bio-Inoculator.

"You two took enough time to use those things," Encizo complained through clenched teeth as he bound one of the unconscious sentries with unbreakable plastic riot cuffs.

"Had to get a clear shot," McCarter replied in a low voice. "These blokes just weren't being very obliging, don't you know."

"They obliged us to a degree," Hahn whispered, binding the other guard. "They confirmed that we've got the right place. The *Altinkaz* has a load of heroin on board."

The warehouse door opened and a young Turk stepped outside with a cup of coffee in each hand. His eyes bulged in horror when he found the two sentries on the ground, surrounded by four strangers. Manning pointed his B-I pistol at the Turk. The kid dropped both coffee cups and raised his hands.

Hahn hastily closed the door. Encizo seized the Turk from behind, twisting the guy's arm into a hammerlock and clamping a hand over his mouth. Manning aimed carefully and shot a sleep dart into the youth's upper thigh. The Turk struggled feebly for a few seconds until the thorazine took effect. Encizo lowered the unconscious kid to the ground.

Katz, James and Ahmed approached the warehouse. The big Turk was burdened with two H&K MP-5A3 machine pistols, as well as his own NATO G-3 rifle. James and Katz were armed with their Uzis and M-76 choppers. The Israeli nodded his approval to the other men.

Ahmed handed the two machine pistols to Hahn and Encizo. Both weapons were equipped with silencers. McCarter slid his Bio-Inoculator into a hip holster and unslung his M-10 Ingram from a shoulder. The Briton then followed James around the warehouse, while Katz and Manning circled the building from the opposite side.

"Let's see who's watching the store," Hahn whispered, working the bolt of his MP-5A3.

"After you," Encizo replied as he prepared for action.

15

Karl Hahn opened the door and slipped inside the warehouse, closely followed by Rafael Encizo and Ahmed. They entered a large storage room. Stacks of wooden crates and piles of canvas bags formed long columns that divided the room.

Half a dozen men formed a line by the bags. They passed what appeared to be sacks of grain down the line to a forklift at the rear door. Hahn approached the laborers and aimed his gun at the group.

"Dur!" he snapped in a hard voice.

The men stopped working. They stared at the German's gun and raised their arms in surrender.

Hahn cautiously drew closer. "Where is Deniz?" he demanded.

"On the ship," a worker replied quickly. "We just work for him. Don't blame us for anything the captain has done...."

A Turkish smuggler surreptitiously emerged from a tiny office, a double-barreled shotgun in his fists. He crouched behind a row of crates and stealthily began to move into position to ambush Hahn. However, Encizo was watching for just such treachery.

The Cuban saw the shotgunner approach. He poked his H&K around the edge of a crate and triggered the machine pistol. The silenced death merchant coughed harshly. Three 9mm slugs punched through the gunman's chest, and the Turk fell to the floor. A muscle reaction caused his finger to jerk against a trigger. The shotgun roared like a mini-Howitzer within the warehouse.

The explosion startled the terrorists. They reacted like cornered beasts—violently. One of the warehouse workers desperately charged Karl Hahn, hoping to disarm the German agent. Hahn's H&K rasped. Three Parabellums smashed the Turk's face and blasted a messy exit where the back of his skull used to be.

Another terrorist grabbed a grain sack and hurled it at Hahn. The BND operative grunted when the heavy bag struck his chest and bowled him over. Canvas split open, spilling white powder across the floor. The MP-5A3 was knocked from Hahn's grasp and slid beyond reach.

"Donnerwetter," the German cursed as he gazed up to see two knife-wielding smugglers lunge toward him.

Ahmed's G-3 assault rifle snarled. A volley of 7.62mm projectiles chopped into the smugglers before either man could use his knife on Hahn. The force of the multiple high-velocity slugs hurled the thugs into a stack of grain bags. Their corpses fell beside the amazed, and greatly relieved, Karl Hahn.

Another smuggler crept up behind Ahmed and attacked, planning to bury the tip of a steel stevedore hook in the big man's broad back. Ahmed caught a slight movement via the corner of an eye. With surprising speed for such a large man, Ahmed whirled to confront his assailant.

The hook struck Ahmed's G-3 rifle and snagged the frame. Desperate, the smuggler pulled hard, trying to yank the NATO chopper out of Ahmed's hands. He might as well have tried to play tug-of-war with Mount Everest.

Larger and stronger than his opponent, Ahmed easily held on to the blaster. However, the big Turk did not waste time struggling with his adversary. Instead of resisting, Ahmed swiftly moved with the smuggler's pull.

The horrified aggressor cried out. Ahmed rushed forward. The big Turk slammed into his opponent and drove the smuggler backward into a wall. The silent giant thrust his forehead into the smaller man's face. The powerful head butt drove the back of the smuggler's skull against the wall hard. Bone crunched. Ahmed released the smuggler, who slid to the floor. A long crimson smear on the wall marked his progress.

Karl Hahn had started to get to his feet when another knife-wielding smuggler attacked. The German immediately scooped up a fistful of white powder from the ruptured bag and hurled it into the Turk's face.

The assailant cursed as powder stung his eyes. He blindly lunged at Hahn. The German easily avoided the knife thrust and swung a fist against the side of his opponent's head.

The punch knocked the smuggler to his knees, but the Turk pivoted and slashed out with his knife, trying to keep Hahn at bay. The German agent had already moved farther away from his opponent. He reached inside his jacket and drew the Walther P-5 from his shoulder leather.

"Allaha ismarladik," Hahn told the smuggler. "Goodbye."

He aimed the pistol at the horrified Turk's face and squeezed the trigger. A 115-grain Parabellum slug pierced the smuggler's right eyeball and sliced through his brain like a copper-jacketed meteor.

Rafael Encizo followed two smugglers who fled to the rear of the warehouse. The Cuban stopped them hard, raking the pair with 9mm slugs. Bullets snapped vertebrae and severed spinal cords. The smugglers tumbled forward and fell into the mysterious realm of the dead.

"Ee-ya!" a voice echoed against the warehouse ceiling.

A figure suddenly pounced from the top of a stack of crates. The Turkish savage literally dove into Encizo. Both men fell against a wall. The Cuban was stunned by the unexpected attack, but he still saw the glitter of a long, curved blade in his attacker's fist.

His heart raced. Encizo's left hand shot out and seized the smuggler's wrist before the guy could use his knife. The Turk's other hand tried to wrench the H&K machine pistol from Encizo's grasp. Warrior and smuggler struggled briefly, until the Turk managed to ram a knee into Encizo's groin.

The Cuban gasped as hot agony bolted up from his crotch. The pain traveled along branches of nerves and seemed to claw at his spine. The smuggler yanked the MP-5A3 from Encizo's fingers, and the H&K fell at their feet. As the pair continued to struggle for their lives, the gun was kicked across the floor.

Encizo still held on to the smuggler's wrist to ward off the knife blade. His other hand raked the Turk's face, nearly gouging out an eyeball. The smuggler cried out as nails ripped flesh. The Turk twisted his head aside and grabbed Encizo's sleeve to try to keep the Cuban from tearing at his features.

A boot tripped Encizo. He fell to the floor with the smuggler on top of him. The breath was knocked from Encizo's lungs. Lights burst in front of his eyes and his head seemed to wobble loose from its neck. Yet he kept his left hand locked around the terrorist's wrist. He was rapidly losing strength and the blade was slowly moving closer to his throat.

The smuggler knew he had the upper hand. Although blood trickled from his torn cheek, the Turk smiled. He pushed harder, determined to drive the knife into Encizo's flesh.

The Phoenix Force pro had to act fast or forfeit his life. Encizo bent a knee and swung it into the smuggler's lower back. The Turk grunted. Encizo delivered another knee lift and hit the goon in a kidney.

The smuggler shifted his body to try to avoid the knee kicks. Encizo's right arm slithered forward. His hand found the haft of a Gerber Mark I in an ankle sheath. He quickly drew the knife and stabbed its 5-inch, double-edged blade under the smuggler's right arm.

The Turk screamed as sharp steel plunged into the sensitive armpit. The smuggler's hand opened and his knife fell. It clattered on the floor near Encizo's ear.

The Cuban shoved his opponent aside. The smuggler was paralyzed by shock and internal bleeding caused by massive damage to nerves and veins. Encizo climbed to his feet. The room seemed to weave before his eyes and his legs felt weak and unsteady. His genitals still throbbed painfully.

Encizo gathered up his machine pistol just as two shapes appeared at the end of a column of crates. The Cuban raised his H&K blast machine but held his fire.

"Easy, my friend," Karl Hahn urged as he and Ahmed approached. "The battle is over."

The Cuban heard the roar of machine gunfire and exploding grenades outside the warehouse. He reached inside his jacket and fished out a fresh magazine for his MP-5A3.

"Not quite," Encizo remarked grimly. "It sounds like the rest of the team may still need some help."

THE OTHER FOUR MEMBERS of Phoenix Force had moved into position at both sides of the warehouse in order to cover the pier and the *Altinkaz*. When shooting erupted within the building, more than a dozen figures quickly appeared on the decks of the docked ship. Several men armed with an assortment of weapons charged down the gangplank to assist their comrades in the warehouse.

Colonel Katzenelenbogen aimed his Uzi and opened fire. The silencer-equipped subgun barked softly as the Israeli hosed the gunmen with 9mm death. Four smugglers collapsed, blood spurting from bullet holes in their chests and faces.

David McCarter hit the two remaining gunmen with a volley of Ingram slugs. The smugglers convulsed and screamed as Parabellum projectiles burrowed into flesh. The pair tumbled to the pier. A pool of blood began to form beneath the cluster of fresh corpses.

"*Suraya bakin!*" a voice shouted from the deck of the *Altinkaz*. "Over there!"

A number of smugglers on board the ship pointed toward McCarter's position. The Briton did not have a silencer on his Ingram, so both the noise and the muzzle flash attracted more attention than Katz's Uzi. The English commando retreated for cover as a number of full and semiautomatic firearms snarled. Bullets tore chunks of wood from the corner of the warehouse.

"Bloody hell," McCarter growled, examining a crimson blotch on the back of his right hand.

"You've been hit," Calvin James said as he reached for the medic kit on his belt.

"It'll keep, mate," the Briton assured him. "Just a splinter this time."

James craned his neck to get a better look at Mc-Carter's wound. The Briton never made much of a fuss about physical injury. He had suffered a flesh wound during the last Phoenix Force mission in Greece and had been unable to join in the final battle on Krio Island. McCarter had taken the bullet wound in stride, but he had complained about missing the battle for a week after they'd left Greece.

The Briton pulled a shard of wood from his hand and casually tossed it aside. James sighed with relief.

The enemy fire was directed only toward McCarter and James. Katz and Gary Manning took advantage of this distraction. They pulled pins from American-made M-26 fragmentation grenades and hurled the mini-bombs at the *Altinkaz*. Both grenades landed on the deck of the ship near the bow. The twin explosions ripped out planks and shattered glass from the windows of the superstructure.

Men screamed as shrapnel pierced flesh. Three smugglers were hurled over the weather rail by the blast. Their torn, bloodied bodies splashed into the murky waters of the Golden Horn.

Calvin James lobbed a third grenade at the port side of the ship. Another explosion hurled two more smugglers over the rail. The mutilated corpses crashed to the pier. The survivors on board the *Altinkaz* scrambled for shelter.

McCarter broke cover and boldly dashed for the gangplank. The Briton threw another grenade at the bridge of the ship. The M-26 sailed through a window and exploded, blasting the interior of the ship. The *Altinkaz* rocked with the explosion.

The Englishman jogged up the gangplank, his M-10 weaving to and fro like the antenna of a warrior insect. An enemy gunman popped out from the corner of the superstructure and pointed a French MAT submachine gun at McCarter. The Phoenix Force fighter's battle-honed reflexes saved his life. McCarter's Ingram spat fire, and the smuggler's face was transformed into a crimson pulp by a trio of Parabellum missiles.

Manning and Katz also headed for the gangplank, closely followed by Calvin James. McCarter reached the deck of the *Altinkaz*. The Briton jumped over a grenade-shredded corpse and crouched down by the side of the superstructure.

A Turkish gunman leaned over the twisted rail of the fly bridge and aimed a revolver at the Briton's back. The smuggler thumbed back the hammer.

Gary Manning raised his FLN rifle and triggered a quick burst. The would-be assassin screamed as 7.62mm torment drilled through his upper torso. The smuggler tumbled over the rail and dove headfirst to the main deck seventeen feet below.

The Canadian headed for a ladder extending to the bridge. As Manning climbed the rungs, McCarter moved to the port side and cautiously approached the threshold of the superstructure. The Briton took an SAS "flash-bang" grenade from his belt, pulled the pin and tossed the concussion blaster inside.

Voices cried out in fear within the ship. McCarter felt no sympathy for the smugglers. They were part of the international heroin trade and a KGB conspiracy against the entire free world. They deserved whatever misfortune they received. If McCarter had his way, that would be a hell of a lot of misfortune.

The grenade exploded. The roar terminated the

screams of the smugglers inside the superstructure. Mc-
Carter poked the barrel of his Ingram around the corner
and triggered a short burst into the companionway below. At last the Briton crossed the threshold. He descended the steps slowly, his M-10 ready for action.

Five blood-stained bodies littered the companionway.
Two stunned smugglers crawled along the corridor.
Their eardrums had been ruptured by the concussion
blast, but they still held weapons. McCarter's Ingram
erupted and half a dozen 9mm slugs tore into the smuggler's hearts and lungs.

McCarter watched the doors of the cabins that lined
both sides of the companionway. One door opened a
crack. The Briton snap-aimed and fired at the door. A
voice shrieked in reply.

Another door opened behind McCarter. He pivoted
as a figure charged forward. A burly Turk who had
been working in the engine room before the battle began
attacked the Briton. The smuggler was clad in a dirty
undershirt, canvas trousers and about two pounds of oil
and grease. A long steel wrench protruded from a ham-
size fist.

McCarter's sudden movement had shifted his skull
out of the path of the wrench. The tool clanged against
the frame of his Ingram, striking the machine pistol
from his grasp.

"Bugger!" the Briton snarled as he immediately
jabbed his right fist into the Turk's mouth.

McCarter's left hand seized the wrist behind the
wrench before the smuggler could try to use it again. The
English warrior drove a forward elbow stroke to his opponent's solar plexus. The Turk groaned. McCarter hit
him again. The smuggler doubled up, and McCarter's
right arm snaked out to wrap around the man's neck.

The Briton secured a front headlock on the Turk and delivered a short back kick, slamming a boot heel into the smuggler's face. McCarter suddenly released his opponent and whipped a knee under the man's jaw.

The blow sent the Turk staggering backward. A machine pistol bellowed. The smuggler screamed as four 7.65mm rounds punctured his back. The Turk had been shot by one of his fellow hoodlums, who had emerged from another cabin with a Skorpion chopper in his fists.

McCarter instantly dropped to the deck plates before the gunman could fire the Czech chatterbox again. The smuggler cursed when he realized he had killed the engineer instead of the commando. He pointed the Skorpion at McCarter.

The Phoenix Force warrior had already drawn his Browning Hi-Power from its shoulder holster. A champion pistol marksman, McCarter snap-aimed and triggered the Browning. The smuggler's nose vanished in a spray of crimson as a 9mm slug splintered cartilage and burrowed into his brain.

COLONEL KATZENELENBOGEN MOVED AFT along the deck, while Calvin James went forward to the bow. The Israeli discovered a trio of enemy gunmen in the starboard quarter. The smugglers were young and quick, but Katz's reflexes had been developed by four decades of experience.

He had removed the sound suppressor from the barrel of his Uzi because silence was no longer necessary and the device reduced accuracy. The submachine gun roared. Parabellum devastation ripped two smugglers to pieces. Blood gushed from their bullet-ravaged bodies as they slumped to the deck.

The third gunman fell against the weather rail. His

chest and right shoulder had been gouged by 9mm slugs and a Turkish MKE pistol had slipped from his fingers, but fire burned in the wounded man's eyes as he tried to retrieve the gun.

Yakov rushed forward, swinging his prosthetic limb in a fast backhand sweep. Steel hooks smashed into the smuggler's face. The blow sent him hurtling over the top of the rail. The Turk screamed until he plunged into the Golden Horn below.

Two smugglers at the bow had spotted Gary Manning on the bridge of the *Altinkaz*. They aimed Soviet-made AKM assault rifles at the Canadian and prepared to fire. Manning failed to notice the enemy gunmen, but Calvin James arrived in time to see the Turks were about to blast his partner.

The black man's M-76 subgun spoke first. The two smugglers convulsed wildly across the deck as a tidal wave of 9mm rounds sent them on a one-way trip to Davy Jones's locker. James hosed the pair with another volley and sent them crashing through a weakened section of the weather rail.

Two more figures dashed for cover by a stack of crates beneath the long wooden shaft of a cargo boom. James swung his M-76 at the retreating smugglers and squeezed the trigger. The weapon did not fire.

"Aw, shit," he rasped, glancing down at a bent cartridge casing that jutted from the breech.

The smugglers realized the Phoenix Force fighter's gun had jammed. The pair charged forward. One held a Tokarev pistol in both hands. The other wielded a large wood-and-iron pulley at the end of a thick rope. James hastily discarded the S&W chopper and yanked his Colt Commander from shoulder leather.

The smuggler's Russian-made Tokarev cracked. A

7.65mm projectile punched into the wall of the superstructure inches from James's left elbow.

The black warrior had been shot at before. It never failed to scare the shit out of him. Only James's self-discipline and training kept him from freezing up from fear. He aimed the Colt with a steady hand and blasted a .45-caliber bullet into the center of the gunman's chest.

The big 185-grain hollowpoint slug knocked the smuggler five feet. He fell to the deck plates and tumbled back into the crates. The Turk tried to rise. He coughed violently, blood spewing from his mouth. Then he slumped to the deck and died.

Before James could aim his Commander at the other smuggler, the second attacker swung the block and tackle. The big pulley struck the slide of James's pistol. The black man's hand popped open and his Colt hurled across the bow.

"Son of a bitch," James growled as the grinning smuggler approached, whirling the block and tackle like a propeller.

The heavy wooden pulley whistled toward James's head. The black man ducked. The projectile brushed the hairs on the back of his skull but did not connect with a solid blow.

The smuggler prepared a backhand sweep with his flexible weapon. Calvin James did not hesitate. He leaped forward. His body was canted in midair, one knee bent, the other leg extended. His foremost boot crashed into the Turk's face. Bone and teeth cracked from the force of the tae kwon-do flying kick.

The would-be assassin fell to the deck, blood pouring from his crushed mouth. James landed beside the Turk and dropped to one knee. He quickly seized the block and tackle. The black man held the pulley in his fist and hammered it into the smuggler's forehead. Skull bone crunched. Scarlet tears oozed from the corners of the dead man's sightless eyes.

GARY MANNING HAD ENCOUNTERED a handful of smugglers on the bridge. Three Turkish barbarians were too slow. Manning cut them down with a burst of FLN slugs before they could fire a shot.

A fourth smuggler jumped down from the roof of the fly bridge with a dagger in his fist. Crazy, brave and desperate, the Turk lunged for Manning's belly. The Canadian parried the blade with the barrel of his FLN rifle and quickly delivered a butt stroke to the man's face. The walnut stock shattered the smuggler's cheekbone and sent him toppling over the safety rail. His body sounded like a wet sandbag when it hit the main deck.

Manning moved toward a door and peered through its window. Captain Deniz was inside the control room of the bridge. A stocky man dressed in dark blue uniform with a matching cap, Deniz was crouched by the control console. The smuggler captain did not carry a gun. He had armed himself with the only weapon available—a Mayday flare pistol.

The Canadian wanted Deniz alive. Yet he could not simply storm into the control room. A flare pistol was not a sophisticated weapon, but it was devastating at extremely close range. Manning could not lob a concussion grenade into the room because the explosion would certainly kill Deniz in such a confined area.

Manning was still puzzling the situation when Captain Deniz saw him at the door. The Turk raised the flare pistol. His hand shook violently. Manning quickly swung his FLN forward. The barrel shattered glass as the Canadian aimed the assault rifle at Deniz.

"Drop it!" Manning ordered. He repeated the command in French. "It's all over now. Surrender or I'll just have to blow your brains out, Captain."

Deniz growled something in Turkish and thrust his arm forward to point the flare gun at Manning. The Canadian had no choice. He squeezed the trigger of his FLN. A 7.62mm copper-jacketed missile split the Turk's forehead just above and between the eyes.

The captain's corpse crumpled to the floor. His fist was jarred by the fall and the finger pulled the trigger of the Mayday pistol. A 25mm magnesium projectile burst against the base of the console. Electrical wires crackled and flames exploded within the control room.

Manning bolted from the burning bridge. He scrambled down the ladder to the main deck. Katz, James and McCarter had already regrouped and were waiting for him to join them. Encizo, Hahn and Ahmed arrived in time to see the conclusion of the battle aboard the *Altinkaz*.

"Looks like we missed the main event," Encizo remarked, gazing up at the fire that now raged on the bridge.

"Not yet," Katz replied dryly. "The main event won't be until we find the terrorist headquarters."

16

"I hate to waste perfectly good scopolamine on guys who can't tell us diddly shit," Calvin James muttered as he sank into a chair.

"We couldn't be sure if any of the prisoners knew anything until we questioned them under the influence of the truth serum," Rafael Encizo replied as he poured himself a glass of raki.

"Yeah," James agreed in a weary voice. "Hey, what's that stuff, man?"

"I'm not sure," Encizo admitted. "But it has alcohol in it."

"That's good enough for me," the black man stated.

Phoenix Force, Karl Hahn and Ahmed had taken a few smugglers prisoners. Very few. They transferred the captives to the warehouse by the Bogazici Strait where they had previously questioned Yazod and the other terrorists. However, none of the smugglers knew anything about the powers behind the heroin traffic.

"If only we had Deniz," Manning commented, shaking his head with dismay. "I should have tried to wing him when I had the chance. Maybe if I'd shot him in the shoulder...."

"The bastard would probably have fired his flare gun, anyway," McCarter told his Canadian partner as he used a blade of his Swiss-army knife to pop the cap from a Coke bottle. "In such a confined area that would have killed him, anyway. Forget about it, Gary. It's over.''

"At least we stopped about a ton of heroin from winding up on the market," James said, accepting a glass of raki from Encizo.

"But we're no closer to finding out who the hell is running the dope ring," Manning said with a sigh.

"If you ask me," McCarter began, taking a long draw from his cola bottle, "we ought to make ourselves more visible. With a bit of luck, the buggers will come after us.''

"Oh, Christ," the Canadian groaned. "That's a wonderful idea.''

"What's wrong with it?" McCarter demanded. "After all, the enemy realizes somebody's after them. Remember what happened when we grabbed Noveny? The bastards chased us all over Istanbul. Maybe we can get them to do it again.''

"You've got a death wish, David," Manning told him. "And you want everybody else to die with you.''

"Not *everybody*," the Briton said cheerfully. "Just my mates.''

"That's very reassuring," and Encizo grinned. "But let's see if Yakov and Karl can come up with a plan that will be more appealing than setting ourselves up as bait.''

"I still don't see anything wrong with the idea," McCarter insisted.

"Pass the raki," Manning muttered.

A car pulled into the alley next to the warehouse. All four commandos instantly grabbed their weapons. Ahmed, armed with his G-3 assault rifle, moved to a window and peered outside. The big Turk turned to the others and waved a hand to assure them there was no cause for alarm. He unbolted the door and opened it. Katz and Hahn appeared at the threshold.

"You guys didn't take long," Encizo remarked. "Got some good news for us?"

"No news at all," Hahn replied with disgust. "Don't drink all the raki. Save some for me."

"Your computer couldn't come up with anything on Deniz?" James asked.

"My computer is. . ." Hahn considered a proper expression in plain English. "Fucking useless."

"What does that mean?" McCarter asked sharply.

"Hahn's computer links to both the National Security Service in Ankara and the Istanbul Police Department have been terminated," Katz explained. "His access code number has apparently been erased in both places."

" 'Erased'?" James frowned. "How did it happen?"

"Could it be some sort of mistake?" Manning inquired. "Maybe an accident?"

"Not at both the NSS and Istanbul police headquarters," Hahn replied. "I think the National Security Service is unhappy with us. They've cut off my computer link in Ankara and ordered the Istanbul police to do likewise."

"The bloody NSS isn't supposed to know about us," McCarter complained. "One reason we were sent is because the KGB has a mole in either Turkish intelligence or the CIA."

"Or both," Manning added. "That's why we've been working with you, Karl. You're with the BND and there's no evidence that West German intelligence in Turkey has been infiltrated by the Soviets."

"Just wait a minute," Hahn insisted. "Don't you recall that incident at the airport? How do you think we avoided an inquest? Because I used connections with the authorities. I don't own a used-car lot. All the vehicles we've been using were supplied by the NSS. The BND operations in Turkey aren't large enough to function without cooperation from the National Security Service.''

"Everyone calm down," Katz commanded in a hard voice. "Karl hasn't violated our security. He hasn't even told the NSS where his safe houses are located, let alone tell them any details about our actions. That's probably why the NSS cut him off from their computer sources.''

"They didn't seem to care what we did," James commented. "As long as we took care of the KGB's heroin connection.''

"Maybe they've changed their minds." Hahn sighed. "This could just be a way to force me to make a detailed report to them.''

"What are we going to do?" Manning inquired.

"I'll make a trip to Ankara and see if I can't get this mess straightened out," Hahn replied. "Deniz was our last lead, so unless we can get some sort of clues from the computer banks, I don't know what we'll do now.''

"I've got a suggestion," McCarter offered.

"Oh, no," Manning groaned. "Can we get another bottle of raki?"

ANKARA HAD BEEN THE CAPITAL of Turkey since the nation officially became a republic in 1923 and was perhaps the most modern city in the country. The capital had numerous historical sites, although far fewer ancient wonders than Istanbul. Yet Ankara was probably a better example of the direction in which twentieth century Turkey was heading.

Karl Hahn gazed out the windows of the taxicab as he

rode along Taltpasa Boulevard. Cars and buses filled the streets, typical of noonday traffic found in most modern cities throughout the world. Skyscrapers and towering office buildings extended into the sky.

The German instructed the cabbie to turn right on Ataturk Boulevard. Virtually every major city in Turkey had named at least one street or boulevard in honor of Kemal Ataturk. The late president was buried in Ankara and the Ataturk Mausoleum was one of the most popular attractions in the city.

Hahn told the driver to go south to the Yenisehir Quarter and continue on to the parliament buildings. The cab delivered Hahn to his destination. The cabbie charged too much for the trip from the airport, but Hahn did not argue with the driver.

The BND agent walked two blocks from the parliament to the National Security Center. After enduring the usual rigmarole about security clearances, he finally met with General Yildiz.

A heavyset man with a shaved bullet head and black handlebar mustache, Yildiz looked more like the Hollywood stereotype of a Turkish villain than the head of the internal-affairs section of the National Security Service. Yildiz was a hard-nosed soldier who had participated in all three military coups since the end of World War II. Fiercely patriotic and totally dedicated to protecting Turkey from anyone or anything that might threaten the new republic, the general was an ideal choice as chief of his department.

Yildiz sat in a huge leather armchair behind his great ebony desk as he listened to Hahn's story. He picked up a gold cigarette lighter and fired a Turkce Hususi. The general watched the smoke rise to the ceiling as Hahn continued his tale.

"Lieutenant Colonel Dimitri Sokmak must object to how you're handling this business, Herr Hahn," Yildiz stated. "These five mystery friends of yours have caused him a certain amount of concern."

"'Sokmak'?" Hahn frowned. "I've never heard of him. Isn't Tren still case officer of Istanbul operations?"

"Colonel Tren was transferred to the East Province to investigate some trouble with the Kurds," the general explained. "Some outfit called the Kurdish Independent Front is raising hell there."

"Tren didn't object to how we were handling our mission," the German remarked. "Why is Sokmak upset? Why did he cut me off from the main computer banks?"

"You can ask him yourself," Yildiz told him. "The colonel will be here any minute now."

"Very well." The BND agent nodded. "I'll wait for him."

"You won't have to wait very long, Herr Hahn," a voice declared dryly.

Lieutenant Colonel Sokmak stood in the doorway. An athletic man with a lean waist and broad shoulders, Sokmak was quite fit for a man in his midforties. His dark eyes narrowed as he stared at the German.

"Having computer problems, Herr Hahn?" the colonel inquired.

"Thanks to you," Hahn replied simply.

"Indeed," Sokmak admitted. "In fact, I came to Ankara to make certain your access code had been erased so you wouldn't be able to tap into the headquarters information banks."

"Herr Hahn says his group is on the threshold of discovering the whereabouts of a base of operations of a major heroin syndicate run by the KGB," General Yildiz stated. "That sounds like a good reason to cooperate with our BND ally. But it seems you've elected to do quite the opposite, Colonel. I'd like to hear your reason for this.''

"Cooperation should be mutual, *evet*?'' Sokmak replied. "Hahn hasn't bothered to tell us any details about those five mercenaries who suddenly arrived in Istanbul three days ago.''

"They're not mercenaries,'' Hahn corrected.

"So you've said before,'' the colonel remarked. "But you still haven't told us who they are or who they work for.''

"I'm not certain of that myself,'' Hahn confessed. "But I know they're on our side. . . .''

"Perhaps we'd be better off if they were not on our side,'' Sokmak mused.

"Believe me, Colonel.'' Hahn smiled thinly. "You would not want to have those five for enemies.''

"Oh, we know they're good at killing people,'' Sokmak remarked. "That's not exactly welcome news in Turkey these days. Do you know how difficult it has been to restore and maintain law and order in Turkey? You weren't here in the seventies, when violence and terrorism threatened to tear our nation apart.''

"I'm aware of that,'' the German assured him.

"Really?'' The colonel raised his eyebrows. "Your friends have certainly been involved in enough violence since they arrived. There was a full-scale gun battle at the airport within minutes after they got off their plane. A police officer was killed in the fight.''

"The terrorists murdered that officer,'' Hahn stated. "I made a complete report about the incident.''

"Hardly 'complete,' considering the lack of information you saw fit to give about the foreigners,'' Sokmak said stiffly. "And you haven't bothered to make any more reports since. That gun battle at the Sandalye Furniture Factory was their handiwork, wasn't it?''

"Nobody got hurt except some terrorists," Hahn said with a shrug.

"Then you admit you and your five comrades were responsible?" the colonel asked.

"Why should I be ashamed of it?" the German replied mildly. "We also delivered an Iranian zealot named Yazod and a couple of other terrorist survivors to a hospital emergency section. The Istanbul police have posted sentries at the terrorists' rooms until they're healthy enough to go to jail.''

"You think that justifies your actions?" Sokmak demanded. "What about that high-speed chase through the middle of Istanbul yesterday? That was your friends again, correct?''

"No innocent bystanders were harmed," the German told him.

"And last night," Sokmak continued. "There was another terrible battle at a harbor along the Halic. A cargo vessel was burned and bodies were littered all over the pier.''

"Have you ever tried to arrest a terrorist, Colonel?" Hahn asked. "They usually won't come along peacefully. They're highly dangerous fanatics who regard mayhem and murder to be methods of political procedure. You don't deal with terrorists as one does most criminals.''

"Did you use this same defense to justify your personal vendetta against the German Red Army when you were a member of the GSG-9 unit in your own country, Hahn?" Sokmak sneered. "I know all about you, Hahn. The BND sent you to Turkey because they didn't want you to remain in Germany. Your vigilante behavior might be an embarrassment. So we get stuck with you here.''

''Your opinion of me isn't an issue here,'' Hahn said calmly, struggling to conceal his anger.

''I also think I know something about those five mercenaries, or whatever they call themselves,'' Sokmak continued. ''Two or three months ago, we received an intelligence report from some of our people in Greece. They had mentioned a mysterious team of imported commandos who were apparently involved in violent incidents similar to those committed by your friends. They may have been involved in the raid on Krio Island.''

''Sounds like you're grasping for straws, Colonel.'' Hahn shrugged. ''But what if the rumors are true and these are the same five men? Krio Island was a terrorist base.''

''Gentlemen,'' General Yildiz cut into the discussion, ''I've listened to you both for a while now. I have only two questions. One for each of you. All right?''

Hahn and Sokmak waited for the general to continue. Yildiz removed another Turkce Hususi cigarette from a case and lit it before he spoke.

''Colonel Sokmak,'' he began. ''You still have not explained why you denied Herr Hahn access to our computers. Will you please do so now?''

''The reason is obvious, General,'' Sokmak replied.

''If I thought it was obvious,'' Yildiz said in a stern voice, ''I would not ask for an explanation, Colonel.''

''All right,'' Sokmak said, clearing his throat. ''Since Hahn has refused to stay in touch with us or even to let us know his whereabouts, I fail to see why we should allow him access to information when he refuses to cooperate with us.''

"There may be a mole in the NSS," Hahn stated. "I explained that before."

"You don't trust us," the colonel snapped. "But we're supposed to trust you and these five... gangsters."

"Herr Hahn." General Yildiz turned to the German agent. "Have you got a solid reason to believe your mission will soon be successful?"

"Absolutely," Hahn confirmed.

"Do you consider success to be judged by how many people you can kill?" Colonel Sokmak asked dryly.

"Our mission is to stop the KGB and whoever their allies might be from dealing in heroin," Hahn declared. "Nothing less than that can be considered a success."

"That's quite an ambition, Herr Hahn," the general mused. "You must have a great deal of faith in these five strangers."

"I trust them with my life, General," Hahn confirmed.

"These public gun battles are going to cause problems." Yildiz sighed. "Tell your friends to try to avoid that sort of thing if at all possible."

"Yes, sir." The German nodded.

"Colonel Sokmak," Yildiz began, "you will order the computer personnel to reprogram those machines to put Herr Hahn's access code back in the ROM channels of the information banks. Don't correct me if I got the computer jargon incorrect. You know what I want. Do it."

"Yes, sir," Sokmak agreed, clearly unhappy about the general's decision.

"You won't regret this, General," Karl Hahn promised.

"I'd better not," Yildiz warned. "I believe that concludes our business for now, gentlemen. There are other matters that I must attend to at this time. Please contact me again if anything regarding this matter develops in the near future. And something had better develop damn soon.''

17

General Yildiz had clearly dismissed Karl Hahn and Colonel Sokmak. The German and the Turkish intel officer stepped into the corridor outside the general's office. Hahn was surprised when Sokmak extended a hand.

"Let's not be on bad terms, Herr Hahn," the colonel urged. "We are, after all, on the same side. *Evet?*"

"Of course, Colonel," Hahn replied, shaking the Turk's hand. "And I hope you understand that I'm not being coy with you or anyone else in the service. I really know very little about the five foreigners, except that they are the most remarkable antiterrorists I've ever seen."

"So that's what they are." Colonel Sokmak smiled.

"It's as good a title as any," Hahn said.

"If you'd care to use our computers here at the center," Sokmak offered, "I'd be happy to take you there and have our technicians reprogram approval of your access code so you may use the machines immediately."

"Tesekkur ederim," Hahn answered, considering the offer. "Thank you, but I'd better get back to Istanbul and discuss some matters with the others."

"Very well," Sokmak agreed. "I'm glad we've straightened out any misunderstanding between us, *mein Herr*."

Karl Hahn left Colonel Sokmak in the hallway and

headed for the closest exit. He did not trust Sokmak's sudden change of attitude. Hahn had been an intelligence officer long enough to be suspicious of anyone in the same field regardless of which side they worked for. Deceit was part of the business.

The offer to use the computers in the center had not been the bighearted gesture that Sokmak wanted it to appear to be. He had probably made the offer because he wanted to look over Hahn's shoulder—one way or the other.

Perhaps the BND agent had misjudged Colonel Sokmak, but he did not intend to take any risks with security of the mission. Hahn did not care if Sokmak's offer had been given in good faith. The German had learned that he could never truly trust anyone. He had often regretted trusting others in the past, but he had never been sorry for distrusting anyone.

Hahn left the National Security Center and headed for the parliament buildings, where one could always find a number of taxicabs waiting for customers.

Three men suddenly emerged from an alley next to a coffee shop. The trio were clad in shabby jellabas and goatskin boots. Each man wore a dark-green turban with a scarf drawn over his face. They appeared to be mountain Kurds, although Hahn realized the trio might have chosen the clothing simply to disguise their appearance.

The trio blocked Hahn's path. He saw the bone handles of knives sheathed on their belts. The German was not armed. He had flown to Ankara via a commercial airline and thus had been unable to bring his trusted Walther P-5 pistol. As Hahn backed away from the trio, a hard metal cylinder poked against the small of his spine.

"Move and you die," a voice whispered at Hahn's ear. The pistol muzzle dug harder at his back.

"That's a melodramatic threat," Hahn replied dryly, raising his hands to shoulder level.

"Lower your hands!" the gunman rasped.

Hahn tried to ignore the throbbing pulse under his ear and the wild rhythm of his racing heart. He tried to evaluate the situation as rapidly and calmly as possible. The four hoodlums had him cold, but they obviously wanted him alive.

They might be reluctant to kill him in broad daylight on a sidewalk located between the National Security Center and the Turkish parliament. If they hesitated, Hahn might have a chance.

"I told you to lower your hands," the gunman growled.

The German obeyed. He lowered his arms slowly, then suddenly pivoted to the right. He lashed a karate chop at the gunman's weapon. A small-caliber pistol popped like a firecracker. Hahn heard one of the masked trio cry out in pain as the bullet struck flesh.

Hahn swung a left hook to the gunman's face. The hoodlum's head bounced back from the punch and his scarf slipped from his face to reveal a snoutlike nose and rodent front teeth. Hahn's right hand seized the wrist behind the man's little Italian automatic. His left hand gripped the guy's throat as he twisted the gun toward the other three assailants.

One of the masked trio had doubled up, a .25-caliber slug in his belly. The other two stood back, unwilling to suffer the same fate as their comrade. Hahn shoved the gunman's wrist to aim the little pistol at the closest Kurd.

Then the gunman opened his fist and dropped the .25 auto. Hahn cursed under his breath as the two uninjured opponents charged forward.

The German agent quickly shoved the gunman into

one of the advancing Kurds. Both hoodlums fell backward into the coffee shop.

Another masked goon lunged at Hahn. The BND man snap-kicked the attacker in the groin. The Kurd folded up with a choking gasp. Hahn clashed both hands together and swung them into his opponent's face. The powerful blow propelled the killer four feet. He fell against the hood of a car and slumped unconscious in the gutter.

Despite the bullet in his stomach, the wounded Kurd had not been put out of action. The tiny .25 slug lacked both size and velocity to put a man down. The thug clutched his belly with one hand while the other reached for the haft of his knife. Hahn punched him in the face before he could draw his weapon. The Kurd collapsed on the sidewalk.

The third masked assailant swung a wild knife slash at Hahn. The German ducked under the whirling blade and drove a fist into the man's solar plexus. He quickly caught the wrist behind the goon's knife and slid his other hand between the Kurd's legs.

Hahn picked the man up in a crotch lift. The Kurd screamed as Hahn heaved him headfirst through the front window of the coffee shop. Glass exploded, and the hoodlum plunged into the shop and crashed onto a tabletop. The furniture tipped over, dumping his senseless form to the floor.

Alarmed patrons within the coffee shop shouted an assortment of colorful Turkish oaths. Hahn turned from the shattered window and saw the blur of a slashing arm. Something hard slammed into the side of his head an inch above the vulnerable temple. A painful white light burst inside his skull. Karl Hahn felt himself fall into a black limbo. . . .

18

The pungent odor of ammonia filled Karl Hahn's nostrils. He turned his head from the foul odor. Shards of hot metal seemed to jab his brain. The pain wrenched an involuntary groan from the BND agent.

"He's awake," a voice echoed from somewhere outside Hahn's throbbing skull. "Aren't you, German pig!"

A palm swatted the side of Hahn's face. The blow felt as if it drove chips of sharp stone into his cheek. Consciousness returned abruptly. Hahn gazed up at the leering ratlike face of his tormentor.

Hahn tried to move his arms, but his wrists were bound together at the small of his back. His ankles were also bound. The German was lying on a worn-out mattress that stank of mildew. A kerosene lantern swung from a hook in the ceiling.

"You Germans still think you are the master race?" The Turkish thug smiled. He raised a hand in a stiff arm salute. "*Sieg Heil,* Aryan scum."

"I'm not a damn Nazi," Hahn growled hoarsely. "Hitler was dead before I was born."

"Scratch a German," Rat Face sneered, "find a Nazi."

"Look in a mirror and scratch yourself," Hahn suggested. "You'll get to see a man-sized maggot."

Rat Face smashed the back of his hand across Hahn's

mouth. The German tasted blood, but he merely smiled up at the Turk.

"Why don't you untie me and we'll see who can hit harder," Hahn invited.

The hood balled his fist and prepared to strike Hahn again. A curt voice shouted, *"Hayir, Jabari!"*

"Is that you, Colonel Sokmak?" Hahn inquired, trying to see past the hood.

"How did you guess?" Colonel Sokmak asked as he approached Hahn.

"It was easy enough to figure you must have sent those four idiots to abduct me," the German replied. "It was obviously a rush job. Broad daylight on a public street, no silencer on the gun and wearing masks. *Gott!* How clumsy."

"We caught you, didn't we?" Jabari, the rat man sneered.

"It wasn't a brilliant kidnapping," Sokmak admitted. "But we couldn't allow you to return to Istanbul."

"There were certainly witnesses to my abduction," Hahn stated. "Someone will report it."

"And they'll believe three Kurds kidnapped you," Sokmak said with a shrug.

"You want the Kurds to be blamed?" Hahn frowned. "And you didn't become the chief case officer of NSS operations in Istanbul until Colonel Tren was transferred to the East Province to deal with the Kurdish Independent Front."

"You have a good memory, Hahn." Sokmak nodded. "Now can you put the pieces together?"

"The Kurdish Independent Front isn't a genuine terrorist outfit," Hahn decided. "The KGB fabricated it so they could get their mole promoted."

"Very good." Sokmak smiled. "But the Kurdish Independent Front is going to serve more than one purpose. It will increase hostility between Turks and Kurds, which will cause more domestic problems in Turkey. It will also direct the authorities to the individuals who will eventually be blamed for the heroin traffic.''

"You said 'we,'" Hahn noticed. "Then you're the KGB mole. Are you a Soviet spy or a traitor to Turkey?''

"One man's traitor is another man's hero," Sokmak said as he shrugged. "Besides, the Russians have made me a very attractive offer, which is more than the National Security Service has done.''

"So you're a traitor." Hahn spat out the words. "How do you and your KGB friends intend to blame the Kurds for the drug trade? The Kurds don't own any poppy fields and they haven't got enough influence in the cities for something like that.''

"Not the Kurds exactly," the colonel replied.

Hahn wrinkled his brow as he tried to put the mental jigsaw puzzle together.

"Then you're going to blame one of the agas," the German announced. "Some of them still own large amounts of property and a few have hired Kurds to work the fields.''

"My, you are a good detective, Hahn." Sokmak laughed. "All the more reason to abduct you.''

"The agas must be cooperating with the KGB," the German decided. "Whoever he is, the landowner is growing the poppies on his property and probably processing the heroin. If I had my computer, I could probably figure out who it is.''

"You and your computer have caused enough trouble," Sokmak said sternly. "To say nothing of those five mercenary gangsters the Americans sent. That's what really concerns us, Hahn. And you know who they are."

"Just a bunch of guys from out of town," Hahn answered.

"Those five men have already ruined two major KGB operations," Sokmak declared. "One involved the sabotage of nuclear power plants in the United States and the other was the Krio business in Greece. The Kremlin wants those five terminated with extreme prejudice."

"I can see why." Hahn smiled. "I've already told you they're the best I've ever seen. You can kill me, Sokmak, but that won't stop them. Without me and my computers and knowledge of Turkey, they'll be slowed down for a while, but they'll keep after you bastards."

"Not if we get them first," the colonel stated. "And you're going to tell us where we can find them."

"So that's why you wanted me alive," Hahn remarked. "For interrogation. What are you going to use? Scopolamine?"

"Perhaps," Sokmak replied.

"Are you familiar with any of the research that's been done with allergies?" Hahn inquired. "Science has only recently really understood what an allergy is. Since 1969 there have been some fascinating strides in this research."

"What are you rambling on about, Hahn?" Sokmak demanded.

"The BND developed a drug a couple of years ago," the German explained. "When injected into a subject over a period of four months it programs certain biochemical responses within the body. The results last a lifetime."

"What effects?" Sokmak frowned.

"If you inject any type of truth serum into my blood-stream," Hahn began, "any type at all, it will instantly trigger a biochemical response. A strong hemotoxin will appear in my blood and ten minutes later, I'll be dead."

Sokmak glared at Hahn, trying to read the German's expression to determine if he was telling the truth or not.

"I believe your American friends would call that story 'bullshit,'" the colonel declared.

Hahn's face did not betray the fact that Sokmak had guessed correctly.

"So bring on the scopolamine," the German invited.

"We might use torture, instead," the double agent mused.

"I have a very high pain threshold," Hahn replied. "It will probably take two to three days to break me, if I don't die first."

"I have someone who specializes in big tough men in less than eight hours," Sokmak warned. "Would you like to meet him?"

"His company would certainly be refreshing compared to yours, Sokmak," Hahn said, fighting to keep a tremble from his voice.

"Then I'll introduce you to him," Sokmak declared with a reptilian smile.

Colonel Sokmak turned to his henchman, Jabari, and whispered some orders. The rat-faced hood nodded in response. Sokmak crossed the room to a door and went out. The rodentlike Jabari moved to a card table and sat behind it.

"Don't try to free yourself, Hahn," the thug warned as he took the little Italian .25 auto from a pocket and placed it on the table. "If I see you struggle, trying to untie yourself, I will shoot you in both kneecaps. *Anladiniz mi?*"

"I understand," Hahn assured him. "Do you mind if I ask a question?"

"I won't know until I hear what it is." Jabari laughed. "And if I don't like your question, that will be a good enough reason to shoot you in a knee."

"I was just wondering how you got involved in this," Hahn commented as he glanced around the room.

"I've been a Communist since I was sixteen," Jabari replied. "And the Soviet Union is the only hope we have of defeating you capitalists."

"So you trust the Russians?" Hahn inquired.

"More than I trust the military establishment that runs Turkey," Jabari stated. "Besides, the KGB is going to reward me for my services, as well."

I bet, Hahn thought. Jabari and his type were unreliable. The KGB might have a future use for Sokmak, but they would never let Jabari live after he had completed his role in the operation. Petty criminals with half-baked political notions were the most expendable pawns of the world of international espionage.

Hahn found little of interest in the room. The place was bare except for the cot, two folding chairs and Jabari's card table. A carpet of dust covered the floor. The kerosene lamp suggested there was no electricity. Hahn guessed he was being held in an abandoned building, no doubt in a remote area to ensure his captors of privacy.

Jabari opened a magazine and leafed through it, leering at photographs of naked women. He occasionally sipped from a bottle of beer, but Hahn noticed the Turk's right hand never strayed far from his .25 auto.

"Sokmak is taking a long time," Hahn remarked. "He must be having trouble locating his torturer."

"Are you getting impatient?" Jabari inquired with a cruel smile.

"No," Hahn replied. "I'm doing exactly what I'm supposed to do. I'm thinking about what it will be like to be tortured. Torture is half-psychological. I'm wondering what sort of horrors I'll have to endure and how long I'll be able to hold out before I break."

"I'm going to enjoy watching Bicak work on you, Hahn," the Turk declared. "He'll probably start by digging hot needles under your fingernails. Then he might scratch your eyeballs or attach electrical clamps to your genitals."

"Then I don't have any choice," Hahn declared. "I'm going to cheat you bastards of tonight's entertainment."

"What do you mean?" Jabari demanded as he rose from his chair.

Karl Hahn suddenly convulsed violently. His twitching body fell off the cot and crashed to the floor. The Turk rushed forward, pistol in hand. The German trembled slightly, then slumped on his back. His open eyes stared at the ceiling without blinking.

The hoodlum cursed under his breath. He had heard about how espionage agents carry cyanide capsules concealed inside hollow molars. In an emergency, a spy would bite down on the false tooth and kill himself.

"Hahn!" Jabari shouted.

He kicked the German in the ribs. Hahn's body jerked in response, but he did not utter a sound. Jabari leaned over the body, trying to determine if the BND agent was still breathing.

Hahn quickly bent his knees and thrust both feet as high as possible. Shoe heels smashed into Jabari's face. The kick shattered his protruding teeth and crushed his rat-snout nose. He fell, stirring a cloud of dust from the floor. Jabari's .25 automatic skidded across the floor into a corner.

Karl Hahn sat up and sighed with relief. The suicide trick had been risky. The hoodlum might have tested Hahn's response by drilling a bullet through his knee, instead of simply kicking him in the ribs. The gamble had worked, but Hahn's wrists and ankles were still bound and Colonel Sokmak would soon return with his torture expert.

The BND agent tried to crawl. He discovered this was no small task for a man whose hands were tied behind his back and whose ankles were bound together. Hahn tried to roll sideways. His body tumbled across the room until it struck the legs of the card table.

The table tipped over and fell. The porno magazine landed next to the furniture, while the beer bottle rolled to a wall. Hahn crawled toward the bottle and wiggled about until he could place the soles of his feet on it.

He drew back his legs and kicked with all his might. The bottle burst. Shards of glass pierced Hahn's ankle. He almost welcomed the pain as he struggled to turn around.

Hahn sat up and crept backward, using his heels and knuckles. The German groaned softly when a sharp piece of glass lanced a finger.

"Gott sei Dank." He sighed. "Thank God."

The BND agent gripped a chunk of broken bottle and began to rub the jagged edge along the rawhide thongs that held his wrists. He sawed the glass back and forth, keeping the strokes as steady as possible. Jabari stirred slightly but did not attempt to rise.

Hahn felt the thongs break loose. His wrists moved easier. The German continued to saw the bonds with the glass chunk. Another bond was severed. Hahn cut and picked with the glass until he finally freed his hands.

He flexed his arms. Blood circulated through veins

and arteries. The life fluids seemed to burn as they rushed back into his numb limbs. Hahn found the neck of the bottle with a jagged section of glass at its base. The German used it to cut away the cords that held his ankles.

The door opened. Colonel Sokmak stared into the room. He saw Jabari lying unconscious on the floor and Karl Hahn with a piece of a broken bottle on his fist. The double agent reached inside his jacket and drew an MKE pistol from shoulder leather.

Hahn hurled the bottleneck at Sokmak. The colonel instinctively ducked. Glass exploded above his head. He hastily triggered his MKE autoloader. A bullet burned air and plowed into the wall behind Hahn.

The German did not give Sokmak a chance to try again. He charged the double agent and swatted a palm into Sokmak's forearm to deflect the aim of the pistol. Hahn quickly slammed the door, pinning Sokmak's arm against the jamb.

Colonel Sokmak groaned as Hahn leaned on the door. The German seized his opponent's arm in both hands and pulled back with all his might. Bone cracked. Sokmak shrieked in agony. The MKE auto fell from trembling fingers.

Hahn hauled back on the colonel's broken arm. Sokmak cried out again and slumped against the door. His body slid limply to the floor. Sokmak had fainted. Hahn opened the door.

A fist crashed into Hahn's jawbone. He stumbled backward, caught off guard by the unexpected punch. A tall, whip-thin figure stepped over the senseless body of Colonel Sokmak. Bicak, the torturer, drew a double-edged dagger from his belt. A sadistic smile slithered across his narrow, bloodless lips.

"Come to me, German," and the Turk chuckled. "I'm going to show you what I do best."

Hahn dodged the first knife thrust. Bicak executed a quick slash. Hahn hissed in pain as sharp steel split open the back of his left hand. He sidestepped another knife lunge. The German's ankle hit Jabari's prone body and he tripped over the unconscious hoodlum.

The BND agent fell next to the card table. Bicak laughed as he closed in, the dagger poised to strike. Hahn quickly grabbed the flimsy table and hurled it at the torturer. Bicak grunted and snarled with rage when the table struck his chest.

Hahn scooped up the porno magazine and scrambled to his feet. Bicak advanced, his eyes ablaze with murderous fury. Hahn rolled the magazine tightly into a firm cylinder of paper.

Bicak lunged his knife at Hahn's belly. The magazine swatted the blade aside. Hahn's left hand snared Bicak's wrist as he thrust the rolled-up publication into the Turk's throat. The hard end of the paper tube crushed the torturer's thyroid cartilage and caved in his windpipe. Bicak wheezed and gasped until his body quivered in a final death spasm.

Colonel Sokmak rose to one knee and extended his unbroken arm to reach for the fallen MKE pistol. A shoe heel stomped his fingers, crunching bones. Sokmak screamed. Hahn punted his foot into the double agent's chest and bowled him over.

"Confession is good for the soul," Hahn remarked as he gathered up the pistol. "And your soul is going to get a chance to feel terrific, Sokmak."

19

"We had to sit here on our arses while you got all the bloody action in Ankara," David McCarter complained.

"Is he serious?" Karl Hahn asked the other members of Phoenix Force.

"We can never be quite sure about him," Rafael Encizo confessed with a shrug.

Hahn had returned from Ankara and joined the men of Phoenix Force at a safe house in Istanbul. The five commandos were relieved when the BND agent arrived. They had expected Hahn to spend only a few hours in the capital, but he had not returned until the following afternoon.

Phoenix Force listened as Hahn explained the incident with Colonel Sokmak. The German told his story calmly and precisely, as if reading a printout sheet from his computer. The five warriors noticed the fatigue in Hahn's face and eyes, the weariness in his voice. The guy had been through one hell of a night.

"I took Sokmak back to the National Security Center," Hahn continued. "We got there about three in the morning. Naturally, nobody was willing to just take my word that Colonel Sokmak was a traitor working for the KGB. They locked us in separate cells and called General Yildiz. Eventually we managed to get everything worked out. NSS agents checked the condemned building on Saat Caddesi where I had been held prisoner. What they found convinced them I was telling the truth."

"Did you interrogate Sokmak?" Yakov Katzenelenbogen asked, lighting a Camel cigarette held between the talons of his prosthetic device.

"Yildiz had his people do it," the German replied. "And he decided the situation required drastic measures."

"Scopolamine?" Calvin James guessed.

"*Ja.*" Hahn nodded. "You've been using that drug with more skill than the NSS technicians displayed. The scopolamine killed Sokmak."

"That stuff is dangerous." The black medic sighed. "Get the dose wrong by a milligram and it can make a man's heart burst like a balloon in a microwave oven."

"Did Sokmak talk before he died?" Gary Manning asked eagerly.

"He answered one vital question," the German replied. "When we realized his heart wouldn't hold out, I asked him the name of the aga who is in league with the KGB. The man's name is Mustafa Kaplan."

"I assume you ran a computer check on him," Katz said. "What did you find?"

"Kaplan owns a large estate with several thousand acres of land in the East Province, about three hundred kilometers from Buyak Agri Dagi," Hahn explained. "Better known as Mount Ararat."

"'Mount Ararat'?" Manning raised his eyebrows. "That's where Noah's ark is supposed to be."

"A lot of people think the ark is somewhere near the peak of Mount Ararat," Hahn commented dryly. "But nobody has been able to prove it. An expedition brought back some old chunks of wood they thought were part of the ark. Carbon 14 tests determined the wood was less than five thousand years old. So much for solid evidence of Noah's ark.''

"But there were satellite pictures taken of a boat-shaped object in a glacier,'' Manning recalled.

"I remember those stories,'' McCarter commented. "Examinations of enlargements of those photographs proved that the 'boat' was just a dark rock formation.''

"Whether Noah's ark is really up there on Mount Ararat or not doesn't concern our mission.'' Encizo sighed. "But Kaplan's estate might be the key to ending this KGB dope ring.''

"But the agas tend to be very nationalistic,'' Katz mused. "It seems unlikely one of them would willingly cooperate with the Soviets.''

"Kaplan is very bitter about the changes in Turkey since the Atarturk reforms,'' Hahn replied. "To Kaplan's way of thinking, the new republic destroyed his family's dynasty of power. And everything on file about Kaplan suggests that family is all that matters to him. He's seventy-one years old and not in very good health. Kaplan's a widower with four sons and he'd probably like them to inherit some sort of power, instead of just a chunk of property and the Kaplan castle.''

"'Castle'?'' James asked with surprise. "You mean the dude actually lives in a castle?''

"It was built centuries ago by Kaplan's warlord ancestors,'' Hahn confirmed. "And I wouldn't be surprised if we find the KGB there, as well.''

"Kaplan is a fool to form a partnership with the Kremlin,'' Katz commented. "From what Sokmak told you, the Soviets realize they can't hide the source of the heroin trade forever. They're already preparing to arrange for Kaplan to take the blame not only for the narcotics network, but for the bogus Kurdish terrorist organization.''

"The Kurdish Independent Front might be false," Hahn warned, "but Kaplan does have a large number of Kurds on his estate. They're not just a bunch of migrant workers. They're renegades from the mountain tribes. Kurdish bandits have a well-deserved reputation as fierce warriors. Don't underestimate them.''

"Did your computers have any information about the construction of the castle?" Manning inquired.

"Not much," Hahn said with a sigh. "After all, until now Kaplan was regarded as a harmless eccentric, not a threat to national security. However, the castle was built as a fortress. Kaplan has certainly kept it for that reason.''

"Well, we've got the location of the enemy headquarters," McCarter said happily. "Let's go pay them a visit.''

"Yeah," James added with a cold smile. "There's nothing I like better than kicking a pusher's ass, and we've got a whole nest of some of the biggest dope suppliers in the world just waiting to get stomped.''

"Well, before we storm the castle walls," Encizo began, "let's try to avoid charging into our own Waterloo. From the description of Kaplan's estate, there might be more than a hundred terrorists, bandits and God-knows-what-else at that castle.''

"General Yildiz has offered to help us in any way possible," Hahn announced. "He can give us an entire battalion of crack commandos from the Turkish Parachute Brigade.''

"We don't want that many," Katz stated. "If a dozen gunships fly over Kaplan's estate the enemy will be alerted to danger in time to destroy whatever records they might have about where the heroin has been sent and who has or will receive it.''

"Yeah,'' Manning agreed. "And if there's a high mucky-muck of the KGB at Kaplan's castle, he's worth more alive than dead. A guy like that could give us a lot of information about the Soviet intel operations throughout this part of the world.''

"Perhaps,'' Katz mused. "But the heroin scheme is a risky business for the KGB, especially since their case officer has to work directly with Kaplan. The Kremlin wouldn't risk one of their top people for a mission like this. Their agent is staying with a mentally unbalanced would-be warlord and surrounded by terrorists and Kurdish bandits. Too many things could go wrong, and Moscow would realize that, as well. I doubt they'd send anyone higher than a major and probably someone who wouldn't be able to tell us anything we didn't already know if we caught him.''

"To hell with the Russian,'' McCarter declared. "Let's decide how we should hit Kaplan's little fortress.''

"David's right,'' Encizo agreed. "And we'd better do it soon. When the enemy finds out Colonel Sokmak is out of the game, they'll realize time is running out fast. The KGB will probably try to distribute as much heroin to underground operatives as possible and destroy the rest. Then they'll let Kaplan catch hell while they lie low and wait for the heat to die down.''

"And then they'll start the operation again someplace else,'' Katz added grimly. "Well, gentlemen, let's come up with a good plan, and come up with it in a hurry.''

20

0230 HOURS

Phoenix Force was ready to spearhead the assault on the enemy stronghold. The attack force had flown to the East Province in two C-130 Hercules "Super Spooky" gunships. The aircraft were United States military surplus sold to the Turkish government in 1981. Spooky had earned a reputation for getting the job done in Vietnam. Phoenix Force hoped the gunships would live up to their reputation that night.

The gunships landed approximately seven miles from Kaplan's estate. Phoenix Force and thirty Turkish paratroopers continued on to the castle on foot. They came to a halt half a mile from the site.

Calvin James examined the estate through the lens of a Starlite viewer. The castle resembled a scene from an old horror movie...or a nightmare. A moat with crocodiles would not have seemed out of place at the fortress. James wondered if the castle had a dungeon. If so, was it occupied?

"Sentries posted at the minarets," Yakov Katzenelenbogen whispered as he scanned the area with another Starlite. "But the guards don't seem to have infrared telescopes. They haven't spotted us yet."

"All right, lads," David McCarter said softly, working the cocking lever of his Barnett Commando crossbow. "We've got four blokes to take care of. Make sure you do the job right the first time, because we won't get a second chance.''

"No kidding," Gary Manning muttered sourly. He gathered up his Anschutz .22-caliber air rifle and turned to Karl Hahn. "You're certain our Turkish friends know what to do?"

The BND agent had insisted on taking part in the assault. Although Phoenix Force respected Hahn's ability, they felt he had done enough already, and they were concerned that he be fully recovered from his ordeal in Ankara. Calvin James examined the German's cuts and bruises, especially the knife wound on his left hand and the lump on his skull. The Phoenix Force medic decided Hahn was fit for combat.

"All the men understand the mission," Hahn assured Manning. "Two of the best marksmen among the paratroopers are about to get into position."

"What are they using?" the Canadian asked.

"Heckler & Koch G-3 SG-1 rifles with sound suppressors and infrared scopes," Hahn replied.

"I hope they know what they're doing," Manning remarked. "The glare of a weapon's muzzle flash can cause temporary blindness when increased by an infrared lens. Silencers reduce the muzzle flash, but it doesn't take much brilliant light to cause that effect. Feels like a laser beam hit you right in the eyeball. That's why I use the Anschutz and David favors a crossbow for this sort of job. No muzzle flash to worry about."

"The paratroopers are well trained,'' Hahn assured him. "Most of them took part in antiterrorist raids back in the seventies. Several are also combat veterans of campaigns in Cyprus."

"Are you two going to talk all bloody night?" McCarter grumbled, impatient for the action to start.

"We just finished the conversation," Manning replied. "Let's go."

THE CROSS HAIRS FORMED AN X at the center of the sentry's chest. McCarter squeezed the trigger of his Barnett crossbow. The bowstring sang and a bolt hurtled into the night sky. It slammed into the sentry. The steel point pierced flesh and plunged into the terrorist's heart.

Cyanide seeped from the split fiberglass shaft and immediately entered the man's bloodstream. He opened his mouth to cry out, but the only sound he uttered was a rasping death rattle. The sentry slumped from the minaret window.

Gary Manning had the second sentry in his infrared sights. The Canadian marksman fired his Anschutz. The powerful air rifle hissed. A steel dart struck the guard under the chin. The needle point punched into the hollow of the Turk's throat and injected a lethal dose of curare. The second sentry died as quickly and silently as his comrade.

The Canadian raised his hand to signal the others that all was okay. Calvin James and Rafael Encizo rushed forward and ran to the wall surrounding Kaplan's castle. Both men carried grappling hooks and ropes.

They took the ropes from their shoulders and quickly judged the distance to the top of the wall. James and Encizo expertly whirled the hooks and hurled them at the summit. Metal clanged on stone. The steel tines caught on the edge of the wall. Both men tugged the ropes to be certain the hooks were secure.

They scaled the wall, climbing the rope hand over hand as they walked up the surface. Others ran to the wall and waited at the base. Encizo and James reached the top and hauled themselves onto a catwalk.

Calvin James unslung his M-76 submachine gun. He scanned the parade field below, searching for any movement that might mean danger. He was surprised to see a helicopter in the center of the field. Lights were visible in several windows, but no one stirred outside the castle and the smaller buildings.

The black commando was armed to the toenails. In addition to his Smith & Wesson chatterbox and the Jackass leather rig with his Colt Commander and G-96 "Boot 'n Belt" knife, he also carried a .357 Colt Python in a hip holster.

Encizo also watched for activity within the walls. He was armed with an H&K MP-5A3 machine pistol with a silencer attached to the barrel. The 9mm Smith & Wesson M-59 autoloader was on his hip and the Walther PPK was in his shoulder leather. Encizo's pet Gerber Mark I combat dagger was at the small of his back.

"Seems quiet," the Cuban whispered.

"Deader than a bigot's brain," James agreed in a soft voice.

Encizo strained his eyes to try to see the windows of the minarets at the opposite end of the wall. There did not appear to be any movement within them. Hopefully the paratrooper snipers had taken out the sentries.

"Okay," the Cuban decided. "Let's get the rest of the guys up here."

James waved to the commandos below. McCarter and Manning scaled the wall to join their partners. Three paratroopers swung grappling hooks at the summit. The black warrior turned to Encizo.

"Figure we should use ropes to climb down to the parade field?" he inquired.

"There must be some stairs inside those towers," Encizo remarked, gesturing toward a minaret. "Why not do something the easy way for a change?"

"Guess it won't become a habit," James said with a shrug.

McCarter and Manning reached the top and climbed onto the catwalk. The Briton and Canadian had discarded their sniper weapons, but both men were well armed. McCarter carried his two favorite weapons, the M-10 Ingram and Browning Hi-Power. He also had a .38 Special Charter Arms snub-nosed revolver in a holster at the small of his spine as a backup piece.

Manning had his FLN assault rifle and a .41 Magnum Smith & Wesson revolver with an 8-inch barrel in a cross-draw holster on his belt. The Phoenix Force demolitions expert also carried a backpackful of assorted explosives. Naturally, all four men were equipped with grenades and plenty of spare ammunition.

"This is such a lovely night for a raid," McCarter said with a sigh, gazing up at the plethora of stars in the black velvet sky.

"You can write a poem about it later," Manning muttered. "If we're still alive."

YAKOV KATZENELENBOGEN and Karl Hahn had climbed ropes to the top of the wall at the opposite end of the fortress. The one-armed Israeli moved to a minaret and checked inside to be certain the sentry was dead. The terrorist's head had been shattered by three bullets.

Hahn inspected the other minaret and found another corpse. He joined Yakov on the catwalk. The German still carried his H&K MP-5A3 and Walther P-5 autoloader. Katz was armed with his trusted Uzi subgun and packed the SIG-Sauer P-226 pistol in shoulder leather and an Eagle automatic in a hip holster. The Eagle was an Israeli-made .357 Magnum autoloading pistol with an ambidextrous safety catch—an obvious advantage for a man with only one hand.

Ahmed scaled the wall to the summit. The big Turk smiled and nodded at Hahn as he unslung his G-3 assault rifle.

"Karl," the Israeli whispered, "signal the pilots of the gunships. Time for them to carry out their seek-and-destroy mission."

"Don't you think we should wait until we're all in position?" Hahn asked.

"They have to locate and destroy the heroin plant and the poppy fields," Katz insisted. "That's too important to risk any delay."

"If the enemy hears the explosions they'll be on guard," Hahn warned.

"They'll probably know we're here before the gunships blast their targets," the Israeli replied. "Send the signal."

The German extended the antenna of a radio transceiver and pressed a button three times. A small orange light flashed above the button. It flashed again. The gunship pilots had responded to the signal.

"They'll be on their way in a minute," Hahn told Katz.

"Good." The Phoenix Force commander nodded. "Remind the Turks that the rest of our unit is also over the wall. We don't want any of our people killed by somebody on our own team."

Commandos from the Turkish Parachute Brigade climbed to the top and joined the Phoenix Force groups at both ends of the fortress. Ten paratroopers remained on the walls and quickly spread out to form a large horseshoe formation around the castle. The others descended the stairs of the minarets to the parade field below.

The five men of Phoenix Force and their allies moved silently through the night. They stayed close to the shadows of the buildings, using the darkness for camouflage.

The silence caused tremors to travel along their spines like the soft tread of a tarantula. Every step they took sounded too loud. The slight rustle of cloth seemed like thunder to their ears. Pounding hearts became bass drums that would surely alert the enemy to their presence.

Encizo, James, McCarter and Manning led ten paratroopers to the castle. The Cuban stopped abruptly. The caterpillar of men followed his example. Encizo had seen two figures emerge from the building. The pair appeared to be young Turks, probably TPLA terrorists. They were armed with AK-47 assault rifles.

One of the terrorists grabbed his partner's arm and pointed at the top of the wall. He had spotted some of the paratroopers stationed there. However, the gunmen's backs were turned to Encizo and his group.

The Cuban quietly drew his Gerber and flipped the knife to grab the handle in an overhand grip. He glanced at Calvin James. The black man had also drawn his dagger. Encizo nodded. The Phoenix Force pair advanced quickly and silently.

Encizo struck. He pounced the closest terrorist from behind and clamped a hand over the Turk's mouth. Before the TPLA flunky could struggle, Encizo plunged the double-edged blade of his Mark I into the side of the terrorist's neck.

A geyser of blood spurted from the severed carotid and jugular. The Cuban rammed a knee into the small of his opponent's spine and bent the Turk backward. Encizo drove the knife into the terrorist's chest, stabbing the Turk's heart.

The second terrorist whirled and tried to unsling his AK-47 from a shoulder. James rushed forward and swung a high roundhouse kick at the Turk's head. The terrorist weaved out of the path of James's flashing foot.

"Shit," the black man rasped when his tae kwon-do kick missed its target.

Off balance, on one foot, James was extremely vulnerable to counterattack by the terrorist. His instincts and training took over. James leaned forward and purposely fell into his opponent. Both men tumbled to the ground.

The black warrior landed on top of the Turk, knocking the breath from his adversary's lungs. James swiftly jammed his forearm under the Turk's jaw and slashed a sideways knife stroke to the man's exposed throat.

David McCarter moved to the door, his Ingram poised for action. The Briton eased the door open with the toe of a boot. He peered inside and saw a paunchy Turk seated behind a small field desk. The terrorist yawned and turned sleepy eyes toward the door.

His expression contorted into astonishment and terror when he stared into the muzzle of a foot-long silencer attached to McCarter's Ingram. The Turk desperately reached for a Skorpion machine pistol on his desk. McCarter's M-10 sputtered a lethal burst of 9mm rounds. The terrorist's bullet-ventilated body slipped from a chair and fell to the floor.

James and Encizo joined McCarter and covered the Briton as he entered the foyer within. The English warrior moved to the field desk and trained his M-10 on the corridor beyond. The other two Phoenix Force fighters slipped inside.

"So far everything has gone as smooth as a baby's arse," McCarter whispered.

"Yeah," James rasped, "but we haven't really come up against any real opposition yet."

"We'd better get the others inside," Encizo remarked. "Just in case somebody on the wall gets an itchy trigger finger."

The Turkish paratroopers filed through the door. Encizo had been surprised by their style of uniforms when he had first seen the Turkish commandos and he still had not gotten used to working with an outfit that looked as if it had been issued gear from an army-surplus store.

The paratrooper's olive-drab fatigues resembled U.S. Army uniforms from the Korean War period, but their helmets appeared to be reproductions of World War II German headgear. Most of the paratroopers carried NATO G-3 automatic rifles, although a few had Thompson .45-caliber tommy guns or Uzis. American-made Colt 1911A1 autoloading pistols seemed to be their favorite side arm, but some of the troops carried 9mm Kirikkales, instead.

"Did anyone notice there's a small motor pool at the opposite end of the parade field?" Manning inquired. "I counted two deuce-and-a-half trucks and three jeeps."

"No sweat," Encizo assured him. "Anybody who tries to leave in those vehicles will be cut down by the guys posted at the wall."

"I'll take the point," McCarter volunteered.

The Briton led the team through the hallway. The interior of the castle combined ancient architecture with modern additions. The walls were centuries-old stone and mortar, but mercury lights had been installed in the ceiling and the floors were covered with tile.

They found several doors. Rafael Encizo opened his packet of lock-picking tools and went to work. The other men covered him as he picked the locks one by one. One room contained medical supplies. Another was full of canned and freeze-dried food. The third held an assortment of field gear. It resembled the TA-50 room of a U.S. Army supply section. Clothing in various sizes was stacked on shelves. Backpacks, ropes, canteens and other gear hung on the walls.

"This stuff isn't making me very comfortable about our mission," Encizo confessed as he examined the field gear. "It means they've got a lot of people living in this place."

"This gear must be for the Turkish People's Liberation Army," James remarked. "I don't think Kurdish bandits would have much use for most of this gear."

"Neither would an urban terrorist," Manning added. "Looks like training gear to me. If Kaplan and the KGB are using this place for a terrorist training camp, there could be more than two hundred human lice crawling around here."

"Or they might train terrorists here and then send them elsewhere," Encizo said with a shrug. "At least that's what we can hope they're doing."

The team moved to another door. It was made of thick steel and secured by a trio of special padlocks.

Encizo looked at the door and groaned. "Maximum-security locks," he declared. "It would take me almost an hour to open this thing."

"I've got some CV-38 'low-boom' plastic explosives," Manning remarked. "I can blow the door without taking all of us with it, but I can't promise it won't be noisy.''

"This must be an arms room," James mused. "Maybe—"

Three figures suddenly appeared at the end of the corridor. They gasped, startled when they saw the Phoenix Force strike team. Two of the terrorists carried AKS-74 autorifles. The third reached for a pistol in a button-flap holster on his hip.

McCarter's M-10 coughed a quick volley of muffled Parabellum rounds. Two of the terrorists fell backward into their comrade. The Briton dropped to one knee as he hosed the trio with another Ingram burst.

The terrorist with the pistol drew his weapon and fired at McCarter. A 7.65mm bullet sliced air above the Englishman's head. A Turkish paratrooper cried out as the projectile smashed into his chest.

The silencer attached to Encizo's Heckler & Koch machine pistol spat flame. The terrorist's face exploded. He dropped his pistol and fell lifeless beside the corpses of his slain comrades.

Excited voices echoed from the corridor beyond. Boot leather scraped floor tile and the metallic *clack* of gunbolts mingled with shouts and curses.

"Oh, shit," James muttered. "Get ready for the roller-coaster ride. Here they come."

21

Terrorists suddenly charged into the corridor. Half a dozen Turkish Liberation Army savages shrieked battle slogans as they attacked, waving their weapons as if they carried banners instead of firearms. The terrorists exhibited a great deal of frenzied boldness but a total lack of discipline.

Phoenix Force and the paratroopers were ready for them. With professional efficiency the commandos methodically blasted the terrorists. Four TPLA fanatics crumpled into a bloodied, twitching cluster. The two survivors bolted around a corner.

"Silly bastards were bunched together like bleedin' bananas," McCarter remarked, swapping magazines for his Ingram.

"In case you failed to notice," Encizo said as he reloaded his gun, "so are we."

"This corridor is too damn narrow," James added. "We're sitting ducks. There's no cover here."

"You can't have everything," McCarter replied with a shrug.

Boots slapping tile and curt orders in rapid Turkish warned the commando team that more terrorists had joined the pair behind the corner. Calvin James took an M-26 grenade from his belt. The black warrior urged the others to step back as he pulled the pin.

James stepped forward and hurled the M-26. It struck

a wall hard and bounced behind the corner. The commandos covered their ears and opened their mouths to protect themselves from the concussion of the blast that occurred one-and-a-half seconds later.

The grenade exploded. Two shredded corpses were thrown into a wall. Voices screamed in agony and moaned in despair. James dashed forward and thrust his S&W M-76 chopper around the corner. The Phoenix Force hardass opened fire on the terrorists still lurking there.

Parabellum slugs smacked into flesh. James saw a terrorist stagger along a wall, his right arm dangling by a strip of skin. Another man knelt on the floor, both hands clutching his shrapnel-gouged eyeballs. James blasted a volley of mercy rounds into the pair and ended their suffering forever.

"Cristo," Encizo rasped as he joined the black commando. "That was a hell-of-a-fancy grenade throw."

"Nothing to it," James replied, wishing his stomach would calm down. "Corner shot to a side pocket."

"Remind me never to play billiards with you," the Cuban remarked.

Automatic fire roared again. James and Encizo turned to see that four TPLA terrorists had attacked from the opposite end of the corridor. One Turkish paratrooper fell, his torso riddled with gory holes. His comrades quickly avenged his death. A salvo of full-auto hell cut the terrorists to pieces.

"Let's get out of here," Encizo suggested.

"Go ahead," Manning replied as he removed a block of plastic explosives from his pack. "I'll catch up."

"We'll catch up," McCarter corrected. "I'll stay and cover Gary until he's finished here. The rest of you better move."

"Hey, man..." James began, but he knew it was useless to argue with either man. One attribute Manning and McCarter had in common was extreme stubbornness.

"Make it quick," Encizo urged. He turned to Lieutenant Yelek, the OIC of the paratrooper team. "Tell your men to follow us."

"Yes, sir," Yelek replied with a nod.

Encizo, James and the eight-remaining paratroopers jogged through the hallway. They soon approached a stairwell where three terrorists were about to descend. The TPLA goons tried to bring their weapons into play, but the commandos responded much faster. Bullets chewed through flesh and bone. The terrorists tumbled down the steps and landed in a lifeless pile at the foot of the stairs.

The strike team saw two figures approach from the corridor behind them. They turned to face the new threat, fingers poised on triggers.

"Hold your fire!" James cried when he recognized McCarter and Manning.

"Told you we'd catch up," the Briton announced with a breathless gasp.

"And I've told you to quit smoking," Encizo scolded.

McCarter instructed the Cuban to do something that was biologically impossible.

"I set a large charge of C-4 back there," Manning explained. "The explosion ought to make the roof cave in and bury the entrance to the arms room under a ton of rubble. At least the enemy won't be able to get their hands on any weapons stored there."

"They seem to have enough already," Encizo commented.

The thunderous bellow of a mighty explosion caught

the team off balance. A violent tremor that resembled an earthquake followed. The men staggered and fell. They covered their heads, fearful the entire building might crash down on them.

"Christ, Gary," James gasped as he picked himself up from the floor. "How much C-4 did you use, man?"

"Not *that* much," the Canadian replied. "I guess they must have stored some explosives in the arms room. Whatever it was, the stuff was pretty unstable."

"You figured that out all by yourself," McCarter snorted. "You really are an explosives expert, mate."

THE SMALLER BUILDINGS served as billets for terrorists and Kurdish bandits. The sounds of battle alerted them that the stronghold was under attack. Terrorists clad in fatigue uniforms and Kurds wearing green turbans poured outside. They carried an assortment of weapons. Both groups favored Kalashnikov assault rifles, although some carried Czech machine pistols or Russian PPSh-41 subguns. A few bandits still carried British Enfield rifles and German Mausers that were twice as old as the Kurds who owned them.

The paratroopers stationed on the wall had been waiting for this to occur. They aimed their NATO G-3 autorifles at the enemy troops and opened fire. A hailstorm of copper-jacketed death bombarded the terrorists and their Kurdish comrades. Bodies convulsed and fell, writhing in agonized death throes.

A dozen bodies littered the parade field. Most of the corpses were terrorists. The Kurdish renegades tended to be more cautious than the political zealots. Few of the bandits had ventured beyond the shelter of their billets.

"Throw down your weapons and surrender," Major

Pazar, the commander in charge of the paratroopers, said through a bullhorn. "Come out with your hands up or say your final prayer to Allah, Jehovah, Karl Marx or whatever filth like you worship."

The bandits and terrorists quickly stationed their best riflemen at windows and began to fire back at the paratroopers. Three Turkish commandos cried out as sniper bullets struck home. Paratroopers collapsed on the catwalks. One man fell from the wall and plunged to the pavement below.

Major Pazar was furious. He grabbed the bullhorn and promptly ordered his men to blow the enemy billets to hell.

Four paratroopers eagerly carried out Pazar's command. Armed with M-79 grenade launchers, they carefully aimed their "bloopers." Four 40mm projectiles hurtled into the barracks.

The heavy explosive charges erupted with monstrous results. Windows shattered. Walls burst apart. The explosions ripped victims limb from limb. Terrorists and bandits shrieked as shrapnel sliced into flesh to puncture muscle and splinter bone. Veins and arteries were severed. Blood spurted from terrible wounds.

Yet only one Kurd tried to surrender. He abandoned his weapon and dashed outside, holding empty hands overhead. Two bandits and three terrorists shot him in the back for desertion.

"Load thermite grenades," Major Pazar commanded via his bullhorn. "If they continue to resist, we'll burn them."

Many of the terrorists were familiar with the effects of thermite. The liquid fire splashed in all directions and burned anything it hit. It ate through flesh and bone like acid.

The fear of this horror was greater than the terrorists' belief in any warped cause. Greater than their fear of their own comrades. All the other terrorists could do would be to shoot a deserter. Death by a bullet was better than the nightmare of thermite agony.

Only two fanatics were demented enough to insist they continue to resist. The other terrorists solved this problem by simply shooting the diehard zealots. Unarmed terrorists quickly darted outside to show the paratroopers they wanted to surrender.

The Kurdish bandits were not certain what thermite was, but they realized that anything that frightened terrorist extremists into submission had to be more horrible then skinny-dipping inside an active volcano.

Most of the bandits decided to surrender. Two older Kurds did not wish to go to prison. They said goodbye to their friends. With calm dignity, they sat cross-legged on the floor, uttered a brief prayer and shot themselves to death. The other bandits stared down at the splattered brains of the two suicide victims. They laid down their weapons and stepped outside.

MAJOR MIKHAIL BORGNEFF sat at the head of the conference table. He tilted a flask of vodka to pour some colorless liquid into the steel cup that also served as a lid. The Russian gulped down the drink and poured himself another.

Borgneff realized the battle was lost. The raid on Kaplan Castle had been skillfully executed. Somehow the invaders had managed to get inside the fortress walls. They had attacked the castle and the barracks. Most of the terrorists and bandits were either dead or forced to surrender.

He heard shooting within the castle. Some of Kaplan's people were still trying to fight. A waste of time, the Russian thought. It's already finished.

"Comrade Major," Josef Kosnov called to him.

Borgneff turned to see the junior KGB officer at the entrance to the conference room. Boris Suvarov stood beside Kosnov. Borgneff swallowed his vodka and poured himself another drink.

"*Da,* Comrade Captain," the major replied, his speech slurred by alcohol. "What can I do for you, Comrade Captain?"

"We've been searching everywhere for you, sir," Suvarov stated as he entered the room.

"Congratulations." Borgneff smiled. "You found me. I thought this would be the best place to sit and have a nice quiet drink and to reflect on the failure of our mission. I'm not sure I mind, really. I never liked what we were doing here, anyway."

"We have to get out of here, Comrade," Kosnov insisted.

Borgneff glanced up at the younger men. They were both armed. Kosnov, the accountant-spy from the Soviet embassy, looked absurd, dressed in his neat blue suit and tie with an AK-47 strapped to his shoulder and a helmet wobbling loose on his head.

Suvarov, however, no longer resembled a moon-faced innocent lad. His blue eyes burned like cobalt flames. Suvarov carried an RPG rocket launcher and a PPSh-41 submachine gun. A Makarov pistol was thrust in his belt.

"So you plan to shoot your way out of here, eh?" Borgneff chuckled. "There are too many of them and they have the place surrounded. It is useless, Comrade."

"We must try, Major," Kosnov told him.

"Even if you managed to escape—" Borgneff sighed "—where would you go?"

"The Soviet border is to the east," Suvarov declared.

"And it is heavily guarded," Borgneff said. "You'd never get past the Turkish guards. Even if you do, there's no point in returning to Mother Russia. Not now."

"You're drunk, Major," Suvarov snapped.

"True," the senior KGB agent admitted. "But I know what will happen if we return to the Soviet Union. Moscow will not reward us for our efforts in this mission. They'll be too busy trying to cover up any evidence that might connect the Kremlin with the Turkish heroin trade. That means they'll have to get rid of us. They'll send us to some place out of sight and beyond communication. Some place in Siberia, I suspect."

"And what do you intend to do, instead?" Suvarov demanded.

"I'm not certain what to do," Borgneff confessed. "So I'm just going to sit here and get drunk. Care to join me, Comrade?"

"Captain Kosnov and I are leaving," Suvarov declared, drawing the Makarov from his belt. "And we can't let the capitalist gangsters capture you, Major. You know too much."

"I 'know too much'?" Borgneff laughed bitterly. "None of us has ever known anything except what the masters at the Kremlin have wanted us to know. The state has controlled what we could read, what we could hear, even what we could think. How can any of us know too much? How can any of us know anything at—"

Suvarov shot Major Borgneff in the back of the head.

22

Yakov Katzenelenbogen led his team to the main section of Kaplan Castle. The Israeli and Karl Hahn threw M-26 grenades at the massive red-oak doors. The double explosion blasted the doors into a pile of kindling.

Two Turkish paratroopers charged forward. Katz shouted at them to stop. Hahn translated the command into Turkish, but the men had already reached the door.

The harsh metallic rattle of machine gunfire echoed from inside the castle. The impact of a dozen 7.62mm slugs nearly cut the paratroopers into halves. Their bodies tumbled down the front steps like two discarded slabs of butchered beef.

"More grenades!" Katz ordered. "We have to take out that machine gunner before we can enter the place."

Hahn hastily repeated the order in Turkish. The paratroopers obeyed. They pulled the pins from three Mark 11A1 "pineapples" and lobbed the grenades through the jagged gap in the doors. The explosions threatened to shake the building apart. A mangled rifle was thrown across the threshold. A hand still grasped the steel frame. It had been severed from its owner's wrist.

Karl Hahn dashed to the doorway. He entered the castle, his MP-5A3 thrust forward. The German fired his H&K machine-pistol as he dove inside. He hit the floor and rolled to one knee, weapon ready for action.

Hahn found himself in a great hall. Furniture had

been destroyed by the grenade blasts. Paintings were ripped to shreds. The walls were cracked and a crystal chandelier had fallen from the ceiling to shatter on the floor.

Seven or eight corpses littered the hall. It was impossible to be certain how many of the enemy lay dead because their bodies had been dismembered, beheaded and disemboweled by the explosions. Hahn's stomach seemed to revolve from the hideous scene of dreadful destruction.

Suddenly two Kurds appeared on the risers of a massive staircase. They aimed Soviet PPSh subguns at the German. Hahn had been stunned by the gory nightmare before him. He failed to notice the bandits until it was too late. Desperately Hahn raised his weapon.

Full-auto fire exploded. The Kurds jerked and staggered as 9mm missiles hammered through their chests. A green turban hopped from one man's head when a Parabellum slug blasted an exit wound at the top of his skull. The Kurds tumbled down the stairs and landed beside the horrid remnants of their slaughtered comrades.

"You okay, Karl?" Katz inquired. The Israeli entered the room and approached the German. Smoke drifted from the muzzle of his Uzi submachine gun.

"*Ja.*" Hahn sighed with relief. "Thanks to you."

"We'd better split up the unit," Katz stated, glancing about to watch for enemy troops. "Since I can't speak Turkish, the best thing to do is probably send the paratroopers to check upstairs. You, Ahmed and I will inspect the downstairs. Agreed?"

"Agreed." Hahn nodded. "I'll relay the command to Captain Barsak."

Barsak, the OIC of the paratroopers in Katz's group,

led the six-surviving Turkish commandos up the stair-case. Katz, Hahn and Ahmed moved to the next room. It was a parlor with elegant furniture of velvet and ivory. But there were no terrorists or Kurdish bandits lurking there.

The warrior trio moved from the parlor to a pair of ornate mahogany doors. Katz gestured for Hahn and Ahmed to station themselves on one side of the entrance. The German and his mute partner obliged. Yakov moved to the opposite side and extended his prosthesis and dug the hooks into the gap between the doors.

The Israeli took a deep breath and yanked with all his might. The latch snapped and one door swung open. A pistol cracked, firing a projectile through the gap. Ahmed thrust his G-3 autorifle around the edge of the door and blasted a rapid volley at the unseen gunman.

Ahmed boldly charged across the threshold, still firing his weapon. The big Turk uttered a tongueless moan and fell backward into the doorjamb. He slumped into a seated position on the floor.

"Ahmed—" Hahn uttered through clenched teeth. The German thrust his H&K through the doorway and sprayed the room with Parabellum rounds, then lunged into the room, hitting the floor in a forward roll.

Katz braced the Uzi across his prosthesis and peered inside.

The room was Mustafa Kaplan's study. Erkut, the eldest Kaplan son, lay on his back in the middle of the carpeted floor. His chest had been pulverized by bullets. An MKE autoloading pistol was still clenched in his lifeless fist.

Haukal Kaplan, the warrior son who had won the respect and trust of Kurdish bandits, was sprawled at the base of a wall. His face was covered by a grisly mask of blood and pink-gray slime that had formerly been brains. A .45-caliber automatic lay within inches of his fingers.

Bedri Kaplan, the lawyer son, huddled at the corner of a desk. The attorney was not a fighting man. His body trembled as he slowly rose and lifted empty hands in surrender. Tears had formed moist lines on his cheeks.

Bedri had not been weeping due to fear. Katz saw the cause of Bedri's grief. Mustafa Kaplan's body was seated behind his teakwood desk. His head was cocked to one side, eyes staring blindly into oblivion. A bloodied bullet hole at his right temple revealed what his fate had been.

"Kaplan knew he'd lost his last chance to reclaim an empire," Hahn commented. "So he chose the only course that would allow him to escape the humiliation of having the Kaplan name dragged through the mud by an ugly trial."

"That old man was responsible for too much death and misery to deserve any sympathy," Katz said in a solemn voice. "In life or death."

The Israeli kept his Uzi trained on Bedri Kaplan as he glanced down at Ahmed. The big Turk's face was full of astonishment. His mouth hung open and his eyes were wide with surprise. From a bullet hole in his forehead, blood dripped along both sides of his nose.

The dead always seem so startled, Katz thought. He wondered if the final adventure of death would be more amazing than any he had known in life.

"Karl..." Katz said.

"I'm all right," the German assured him. He looked down at Ahmed and shook his head sadly.

"Let's cuff our prisoner. . ." the Israeli began.

Katz heard someone move behind him. He whirled to confront the possible assailant. A large figure charged forward, wielding a long instrument in a two-fisted grip. Steel flashed and a powerful blow ripped the Uzi from Katz's grasp.

His prosthetic arm swung wildly from the impact of a heavy blade. Katz felt the harness attached to the stump of his right arm tear loose. The Israeli jumped back from his opponent, the prosthesis dangling, smashed and useless, at his side.

Ali Kaplan, the strongest and most brutal of the four brothers, smiled at the Phoenix Force commander. The Turkish brute held an ancient Ottoman battle-ax in his fists. Ali bellowed like a rabid bear and attacked the disabled Israeli.

Katz sidestepped from the path of an ax swing and suddenly closed in to seize the haft of his opponent's weapon. Ali was surprised by the older man's strength, unaware that amputees often develop considerable muscle power in their remaining limbs.

But Katz did not intend to grapple with an opponent who was young, muscular and equipped with two good arms. The Israeli slammed a hard side kick to Ali's kneecap. The Turk howled in anger. Katz quickly chopped the side of his hand across Ali's right wrist, followed by a heel-of-the-palm stroke to the left.

The battle-ax fell from numb fingers. Ali was so startled he barely felt the "scorpion-whip" back fist Katz delivered to his face. Enraged, Ali lunged at Katz, his massive hands aimed at the Israeli's throat.

Katz dodged the attack, parried Ali's right arm with a palm stroke and snap-kicked the big man in the lower abdomen. Ali doubled up with a grunt. Yakov slashed a karate chop between his opponent's shoulder blades. Ali stumbled forward into the doorjamb.

Hahn prepared to come to Katz's assistance, but Bedri Kaplan decided the battle offered a distraction that he should take advantage of. The lawyer bolted to the corpse of Haukal Kaplan and scooped up his brother's .45 auto. Hahn pivoted, snap-aimed his pistol and stitched a column of 9mm bullet holes across Bedri's torso from right hip to left shoulder.

Ali launched himself at Katz once more. The Turk threw a kick aimed for the Israeli's groin and swung both fists at Katz's head, confident a one-armed man would not be able to guard against such a three-prong attack.

Katz's boot shot out, striking the edge of his foot against Ali's shin to check the Turk's kick. Ali's left fist whistled past the Israeli's face as Yakov weaved out of its way. The brute's right arm was blocked by Katz's forearm.

All of a sudden the Israeli seized Ali's wrist and ducked under the big man's arm. Katz pivoted quickly, twisting Ali's captive arm. The Phoenix pro kicked one of Ali's feet out from under him, and the startled Turk found himself hurtling head over heels to the floor.

Ali tried to rise, but Katz's right foot kicked him in the ribs. He followed the attack with a left boot-heel stomp to Ali's kidney. The Turk fell face first to the carpet.

Katz suddenly straddled his opponent and promptly sat on the small of Ali's back. His hand snaked out and seized the Turk under the jawbone. Yakov hauled back as hard as he could and dug his heels into the carpet. Vertebrae cracked. Ali uttered a choking whimper.

Katz had broken the man's backbone.

BORIS SUVAROV AND JOSEF KOSNOV had managed to flee the doomed castle by slipping out a window and hiding in the shadows. They stealthily entered the motor pool. Suvarov led his fellow KGB agent to one of the deuce-and-a-half trucks.

"I have the keys," Suvarov whispered. "I thought we might need to leave here in a hurry, so I took the keys a few days ago just in case."

"But how will we get out of here?" Kosnov asked, a tremble in his voice.

"We'll crash the gate," Suvarov replied as he opened the cab door and slid behind the wheel.

"Are you insane?" Kosnov croaked. "The gate is too thick. We'll be killed for sure."

"No, we won't," Suvarov insisted. "I'll swing a wide arch around the parade field to aim the rear of the truck at the gate. Then I'll shift gears to reverse and stomp on the gas. It'll work."

"I don't suppose we have any choice," Kosnov said as he reluctantly climbed into the seat beside Suvarov.

"No," the other KGB officer replied. "We don't."

Suvarov started the engine.

The truck roared forward and rocketed from the motor pool. As the truck sped across the parade field, paratroopers stationed on the wall of the fortress immediately opened fire on the vehicle. Bullets pelted the body of the cab.

Several slugs struck the windshield, smashing a series of star-shaped cracks in the glass. Suvarov instinctively ducked and swerved to the left. Two bullets shattered the window on the driver's side. A 7.62mm projectile tore into the side of Suvarov's jawbone. The Russian screamed as three of his lower front teeth exploded from bloodied gums.

The truck swung in a wide arc, just as Suvarov had planned, but he made the turn too soon. The truck drove nose first into Erkut Kaplan's helicopter. Glass shattered. Metal crumpled and fuel leaked from the ruptured tank of the chopper.

Chunks of metal were dragged across the pavement as the truck shoved the helicopter. Sparks ignited the petrol and the chopper's tank exploded like a fistful of dynamite. The blast battered the cab of the truck and poured flaming fuel through the shattered windshield.

Suvarov and Kosnov shrieked inside their personal crematorium-on-wheels. The truck rolled on until it crashed into one of the minarets. The burning corpse of Josef Kosnov was hurled through the broken windshield to tumble off the crushed hood. Boris Suvarov was pinned to his seat. The steering wheel had been driven into his chest, crushing his breastbone.

THE FIVE MEN OF PHOENIX FORCE and Karl Hahn wearily emerged from the smoking ruins that had formerly been Kaplan Castle. The paratroopers herded a handful of prisoners at gunpoint.

Yakov Katzenelenbogen sighed. Casualties among the raiders had been relatively small, but he felt a terrible loss nonetheless. Eight good men had died. Eight brave and noble warriors against the powers of darkness. The world had too few men of this caliber. The loss of eight righteous fighting men was indeed a cause for grief.

"Oh, man!" Calvin James exclaimed as he gazed at the bonfire in the distance. "Would you look at that!"

"It must be the heroin processing plant," Karl Hahn remarked. "The gunship pilots said the poppy field is located quite a distance from here. They bombed both sites with enough napalm to burn everything to the ground.''

"Now didn't I say this was a lovely night for a raid?" McCarter stated with a grin.

"Maybe you're right, David," Katz agreed. "Some very fine men died on this obscure little battlefield that only a handful of people will ever know about. But they gave their lives for what they believed in, and their sacrifice was not in vain."

"Let's see if we can convince the gunship jockey to fly past that fire so we can all get a better look at it," Encizo suggested. "I know that would sure make me feel good."

"Yeah." James smiled as he watched the flames dance in the shadows beyond, aware the blaze was the final act of a difficult mission that had crushed an international heroin operation. "I never thought I'd say this—"

The black warrior chuckled and added, "Burn, baby. Burn."

The Gar Wilson Forum

This is for Christian Denny, who wrote to Gold Eagle asking for information about Yakov Katzenelenbogen.

The Katzenelenbogen family moved from Russia to France shortly after the Bolshevik Revolution, and Katz was born in Paris. His father was a noted linguist, author and translator. When the Nazis invaded France, most of Yakov's family was imprisoned in concentration camps. Yakov, however, joined the resistance.

The teenage warrior spoke French, English, Russian and German fluently, and the American OSS saw his potential and recruited young Katz for recon and messenger missions. In the guise of a newspaper boy, he frequently peddled his bicycle behind enemy lines to quietly gather information. The OSS called him "the spy with the paper route."

By the end of World War II, many members of Katz's family were dead, victims of Hitler's death camps. He decided to join the Haganah in Palestine and participated in Israel's war for independence. He later fought the Arabs in the Six Day War, a war in which his only son was killed and his right arm injured beyond repair and amputated at the elbow.

Katz continued to serve as an intelligence and espionage agent for Mossad. As part of an agreement between Mossad and the CIA, American intelligence "borrowed" Katz for two years. Katz has also worked with British SIS, the West German BND and the French Sûreté.

With such an impeccable background, Katz was the obvious choice of Stony Man and Mack Bolan for unit commander of Phoenix Force. Thanks again for the letter, Christian. I hope to hear from you again.

Gar

PHOENIX FORCE

#15 The Viper Factor

MORE GREAT ACTION COMING SOON!

Libyan terrorists are holed up in the London embassy of the newly formed African nation of Madaraja, and they've feathered their nest with enough explosives to blow up two city blocks of London's fashionable West End.

When Khaddafi's killers gun down two government officials and three police officers from the windows of the embassy, all of England relives a nightmare of frustration—the murderers are protected by diplomatic immunity, and neither the police nor the crack SAS can move into action.

But nobody is immune from Phoenix Force.

Phoenix Force titles are available wherever paperbacks are sold.

Mack Bolan's

PHOENIX FORCE

by Gar Wilson

Schooled in guerilla warfare, equipped with all the latest lethal hardware, Phoenix Force battles the powers of darkness in an endless crusade for freedom, justice and the rights of the individual. Follow the adventures of one of the legends of the genre. Phoenix Force is the free world's foreign legion!

"Gar Wilson is excellent! Raw action attacks the reader on every page."

—*Don Pendleton*

Phoenix Force titles are available wherever paperbacks are sold.

GOLD EAGLE

Mack Bolan's

ABLE TEAM

by Dick Stivers

Action writhes in the reader's own street as Able Team's Carl "Mr. Ironman" Lyons, Pol Blancanales and Gadgets Schwarz make triple trouble in blazing war. To these superspecialists, justice is as sharp as a knife. Join the guys who began it all—Dick Stivers's Able Team!

"This guy has a fertile mind and a great eye for detail. Dick Stivers is brilliant!"

—*Don Pendleton*

Able Team titles are available wherever paperbacks are sold.

GOLD EAGLE

**You've not read action–adventure
until you've read**

Day of Mourning
Terminal Velocity
Dead Man Running

*These are the three Mack Bolan books in which he
began his incredible new career. No action-adventure
reading is complete without this trilogy. Enjoy your
greatest action experience ever in three linked stories
that hurl the lethal human javelin known as
The Executioner into the heart of world terror.*

A wanton assault on Mack Bolan's command base leaves
his one true love, April Rose, slain.

Fueled by white-hot rage and thoughts of wild revenge,
The Executioner pursues his sacred quest to Moscow,
lair of the sinister spearhead.

Bolan fingers the perpetrator in Russia and follows the
trail of treachery back to the U.S. He rains a hellstorm
of death on Washington, the city of lies, and comes face
to face with the traitor at last—in the Oval Office itself!

"The best of the best." —*Florida Constitution*

All three books available wherever paperbacks are sold or through
Gold Eagle Reader Service. In U.S.A.: 2504 W. Southern Avenue,
Tempe, Arizona 85282. In Canada: P.O. Box 2800, Postal Station 'A,
5170 Yonge Street, Willowdale, Ont. M2N 6J3.

AVAILABLE NOW!
New from Gold Eagle Books

TRACK

by Jerry Ahern

**The explosive new series by the
world-renowned author of _The Survivalist_**

MEET DAN TRACK. . . . He's a weapons master, a
survival expert and a former major in the U.S. Army's
Criminal Investigation Division, where he'd spent
fifteen hard-fisted years doing the dirty work that
keeps democracies free.

Now he's on his own, and he's out to get the terrorists,
saboteurs and underworld hoods who are fighting to
control the asylum called earth. He's a man of action
dedicated to a single proposition: all men might be
created equal, but _one_ man can make a difference.
Dan Track is that man.

#1 The Ninety-Nine   #3 The Armageddon Conspiracy
#2 Atrocity   #4 The Hard Way

Available wherever paperbacks are sold.

HE'S UNSTOPPABLE. AND HE'LL FIGHT TO DEFEND FREEDOM!

Mail this coupon today!

FREE! THE NEW WAR BOOK AND MACK BOLAN BUMPER STICKER
when you join our home subscription plan.

Gold Eagle Reader Service, a division of Worldwide Library
In U.S.A.: 2504 W. Southern Avenue, Tempe, Arizona 85282
In Canada: P.O. Box 2800, Postal Station 'A', 5170 Yonge Street,
           Willowdale, Ont. M2N 5T5

YES, rush me The New War Book and Mack Bolan bumper sticker FREE, and,
under separate cover, my first six Gold Eagle novels. These first six books are
mine to examine free for 10 days. If I am not entirely satisfied with these books,
I will return them within 10 days and owe nothing. If I decide to keep these novels
I will pay just $1.95 per book (total $11.70). I will then receive the six Gold Eagle
novels every other month, and will be billed the same low price of $11.70 per
shipment. I understand that each shipment will contain two Mack Bolan novels,
and one each from the Able Team, Phoenix Force, SOBs and Track libraries. There
are no shipping and handling or any other hidden charges. I may cancel this
arrangement at any time, and The New War Book and bumper sticker are mine
to keep as gifts, even if I do not buy any additional books.

Name	(please print)

Address	Apt. No.

City	State /Province	Zip/Postal Code

Signature   (If under 18, parent or guardian must sign.)

This offer limited to one order per household. We reserve the right to exercise
discretion in granting membership.   166-BPM-PAD4
Offer expires March 31, 1985

MB–SUB–3